Slinkies 2022

Spineless Wonders
PO Box 220
Strawberry Hills
New South Wales, Australia, 2012
https://shortaustralianstories.com.au

First published by Spineless Wonders 2022

Cover image copyright Bettina Kaiser

Editorial assistance by David-Jack Fletcher, Brooke Cantley, Emily Morrison, Nick Markesinis, Christina North and Kathleen Kelly. Production assistance by Brooke Cantley.

Typeset in Adobe Garamond Pro

Printed and bound by SOS Print + Media
Slinkies 2022 An anthology of short stories
1st ed.

ISBN 978-1-925052-93-0 (pbk)

A catalogue record for this book is available from the National Library of Australia

Slinkies 2022

stories

Edited by

Emma Wortley & Ch'aska Cuba de Reed

spineless wonders

www.shortaustralianstories.com.au

Introduction

Spineless Wonders' Slinkies has been publishing new and emerging Australian writers under 30 since 2014, with short stories and novellas of all styles and genres.

In 2022, we had our highest ever number of entries, with over 100 stories from authors all across Australia and some Australian writers living overseas. It gets tougher every year to make our final picks, but we're delighted with our six chosen entries.

As in previous years, some of the authors have a few publications or awards under their belt, but others are being published and working with an editor for the first time ever. Some are studying or have studied creative writing, others have backgrounds in entirely different fields.

So what will you find in this year's anthology? This year we have six stories which really celebrate the art and craft of genre writing. We have a spot of horror, a dash of speculative fiction, a splash of magical realism. You'll find mysterious goings-on, eerie encounters and worlds not quite our own.

We'd like to give a shout out to Brooke Cantley, this year's production assistant, and to our band of hard-working and insightful editorial assistants, David-Jack Fletcher, Brooke Cantley, Emily Morrison, Nick Markesinis, Christina North and Kathleen Kelly.

Happy reading!

Ch'aska Cuba de Reed and Emma Wortley

An Alternative First Recorded Contact with Macquarie Island, if the Penguins were Zombies

Brianna Bullen

July 11th, 1810

At first glance, through a veil of mist and rain, the island seemed inhabited less by plant life, than by animal. There was nothing but wave after wave of sea elephants and penguins of seemingly never-ending variety, all whining and squawking to each other in a cacophony of sound. They were so loud that their cries could be heard over the rabid wind. Visually, they existed as poorly visible movement under a sheet of grey from a distance, taking form only as they got closer to land. Even during the middle of the day, the sun barely seemed to touch the land, the sky thickened by clouds. Still, it was a penguin paradise, for any sealer or sailor looking for a birdy profit.

Captain Frederick Hasselborough had not known what to make of the strange island when he had anchored off the coast. He was experiencing the true sublime, and possibly frostbite. No matter how insulated and prepared these experienced sealers and explorers were, their thick furs and wools were never enough. Thick wolfskin mittens imported from Norway did little to help with the aches in the fingers – Hasselborough didn't doubt they'd all be experiencing purpling flesh. One of his men had

complained that his Jaeger fleece was not enough
to combat the damp. Thankfully, most of them
had brought oilskins, cotton waterproofed
with oil. They had prepared for the experience
of places like Antarctica – all frost and wind –
but even the bone-seeping damp of this island's
surrounds proved a shock to the system.

The cold of spraying water below them, and
the rain descending from above made every
joint and extremity ache. But this was tempered
by the warmth of possibility – of money and
of fame. His brain was calculating every seal
into coin, and the beasts seemed endless. The
penguins, too, could be melted down into oil,
although their smaller bodies would mean more
would need to be killed for the yield a single
seal would provide. Their waterproof feathers
would also prove a bloody pain. But still, oil was
oil, meat was meat, and profit was profit. That
alone was worth the frozen extremities and the

potential for catastrophe that could occur on an unfamiliar coastline.

Thus, he left the *Perseverance* in the hands of his most trusted allies, those who had earned his favour, and left with rest of the men in a rowboat with a smile. With no port, they could not risk crashing their vessel against the coastline.

This close to Antarctica, the chilly winds billowed a man's blood, one had to push on to not feel like it was freezing within one's veins. Sub-zero temperatures burned against faces; noses already aged by sea-salt near flayed under frost. Thick hoods protected the ears, but faces had to turn away from the winds to brace against its whipping force. Explorers needed to push against it, else they would perish. The roar of the waves under the oar were met by sea elephants on land, a howling dirge that encompassed the eardrums. The ocean sounded like a rush of blood through the head when anxious. Hasselborough commanded the men to row, but also rowed himself. It would be folly not to move in these temperatures. The oars were heavy, scratching even through the layer of the gloves he still wore. Any gathering dampness within was a potential danger, and most would rather battle the freezing air with bare hands now than risk the long-term chill of water-clogged gloves. Hasselborough needed whatever comfort he could get as the wind scratched at his face, salt spray of the sea splashing against his beard. They needed to exert all their strength to push through the gusts of wind pushing against their paths. Perpetual motion was the only way to stave off the freezing cold. The clouds ahead were grey and full as seal bellies, rolling towards their dingy rowboat. Hasselborough would be damned if he was thwarted by a storm before ever stepping foot on this new land.

The rocks at the base of the island cut through the waves, and through the veil of mist over the ocean, the island appeared like a dream. What little light they had on hand illuminated the coastline's jagged edges with its searching gaze. It was dangerous, inhospitable. They were lucky to not be slammed against the icy rocks around their increasingly flimsy-seeming rowboat. It was only the focus and skill of the more senior sailors, and the eager strength of the newer recruits, that got them through the onslaught of wind. A sailor's dream and nightmare all at once. The rowboat was eventually pushed between rocks, the men having to give it their all to keep the boat afloat and not veering into either of the jagged boulders, coming to a stop as they pulled into the coast.

'Stay where you are!' Hasselborough commanded his men as he jumped over the side.

He was to be the first man to set foot on the island. No land had previously been mapped in this section of ocean. A new discovery. A legacy, stumbled upon while exploring unchecked ocean between Tasmania, New Zealand, and

Antarctica. The imprint of his boot in the thick, grey sand seared in his memory before the tide could drag the trace away. His smile faded upon seeing a wrecked ship embedded in the coast. Someone had beaten him. Well, he'd be the first man to stand on the island that survived and came back. The spikes of rain pelleting at his beard were threatening to turn into icicles. The men were grumbling behind him as they dragged the boat and secured it on land. Miserable, truly miserable. They were a wretched lot.

'Make shelter. Make fire,' he commanded. At least they could dry their clothes before hypothermia took hold.

There was no one around – no human, anyway – so he *could* lay claim to the island. He wasn't so arrogant to name it after himself, but he would name it after someone he admired – or at least, could curry favour from. Lachlan Macquarie was the current governor of New South Wales, and Hasselborough was a Sydney man. Macquarie Island was pragmatic. The men seemed uninterested in his naming of the land, responding without much enthusiasm as they huddled over the sad fire they had made from the surrounding grasses.

One of the men – Hasselborough had never been bothered to learn the names of the new recruits, only those who had lasted more than one voyage – began telling ghost stories. Tales of curses descending on unsuspecting archaeologists and explorers. There was a polar rawness to the air, and the fire flickered in the wind, casting strange, menacing shadows around them, of creatures dancing in the twilight. Hasselborough would never admit to being a superstitious man – or afraid – so all he did was tell the man to knock it off. Such tales were an embarrassment.

The man jerked his head and stared at him, a dead-eyed stare. 'You're not scared of a little story, are you, Captain? What, you think the seals are going to rise up and take revenge for murdering their kin?'

Hasselborough wished he hadn't said anything. The laughter of his men was almost mutinous. He just shook his head and turned away in an attempt to show he was above their superstitious nonsense, but not before looking to a senior officer with a look that told him he'd need to cuff the man over the head for that disrespect. He had thought he'd ruled with an iron fist, but much as he didn't bother to remember his new crew's name, they didn't seem to remember the respect that should have come with his position. 'It's foolish to believe in ghosts and vengeance.'

Besides, Hasselborough thought to himself, many of them had brought pistols from the ship in case of external threat from other life forms. They'd be fine.

Seals were everywhere. Penguins, too, the waddling birds jumping from rock to rock that Hasselborough almost envied as he struggled to stay afoot on wettened rock. Even making a shelter further off from the seals was no help, the more profitable fur seals shyly scooting away while their larger sea elephant brethren lazily dragged their bodies closer, entranced by the warmth. Faces bobbed in the water offshore like the damned, and then dived back into the depths. Some of the beasts were curious, and none were cautious. A pair of sea elephants engaged in conflict over a watching female reared up in the sand. The beasts moved quickly, mindlessly, advancing into the human's circle, a blur of sand and muscle. Chest against chest, neither beast wanted to give ground, seemingly joined at the rib. The men at the edge of the circle ducked away, knowing they were no match for the stubborn beasts. Kelp and sand skidded into the fire during the frantic movements, making the flames even more meagre. The noise this close was excruciating, like the force of two trees colliding with each other, if those trees could vocalise with screams like a meaty, grounded foghorn, howling over the wind.

Everyone armed took aim. It took a few shots to fell the beasts, and there was a heavy thud as both creatures dropped to the sand. The nose of one rival folded over the face of the other as they slumped, blood dribbling from the nostrils. This didn't stop the commotion – a howling dirge and scream emerged from surrounding seals and seabirds, a cacophony of wings taking off echoed the shots long after they were fired – but the creatures eventually went back to their grazing and business.

Mourning was short. It had not yet been learned. Indeed, the creatures did not seem to know the threat of bullets, nor known enough about humanity to know to fear it. The big, glossy eyes of a baby fur seal stared up at Hasselborough, the little creature staring up at him with the trust and curiosity of a puppy. Its fur would make for a perfect shawl for his wife.

Satiating hunger was just instinct for these creatures. One organism died, the carnivores among them feasted. Giant petrels bloodied their beaks in the bullet holes of the sea elephants' bellies. The vulturous birds were chased off – there was flesh to consume, blubber to melt down, and skin to sell. Still, the birds circled above, like a shadow waiting to descend with the loss of daylight.

The men complained about the birds, particularly the swarms of slow waddling penguins, punting one of the wandering ones out of the way and against a rock, but the birds paid them no mind.

At least, the living ones. The sailors saw no difference between the watery footprint slaps of one bird, and the oiled webbed prints of another. Light was dim, hopes were high, and anything strange was seen as a trick of the mind.

They didn't see the dark red eyes observing them, watching them, melted and seeping into their own skin. Any exposed bone peeking through flesh was hidden in the darkness.

Afterall, how could any man predict their demise in such a tiny, waddling body?

They set up camp a little off the shoreline, stepping between the docile smaller fur seals and bypassing the rowdy sea elephants. Gentoo penguins huddled close around them, the smaller birds nesting on the shoreline in their own colonies, while the wily rockhoppers with their frayed straw eyebrows were tenaciously making their ways up the cliffs. They would never be as mighty and majestic as the king or emperor penguins, nor as large and valuable. But Hasselborough found the white wave of feathers patterned above their eyes delightful. Like the furry eyebrows of a kindly grandfather.

Hasselborough wanted to keep an eye on the *Perseverance*, docked as it was like a peace flag steady and true along the horizon. They stayed as close to the ocean as possible without risking being swept out to sea while they slept. The pattern on the shoreline indicated the tide would not come in that far on land.

Hasselborough soon grew restless. The island seemed like an endless trail of mountains. The ground, punctuated with rock, was otherwise soft and boggy. Veins of water dribbled down the hills. The land was alive. Breathing, trying to expel them. The penguins and aerial birds stayed close but hurried away from their feet. The yawning fur seals and sea elephants did not give them the same courtesy. They tried to walk around the layers of lazing bodies, not wanting to get muddy footprints on fur they would soon be skinning. But even this was fraught with peril.

Rocky nests were everywhere. What vegetation there was – nothing Hasselborough would consider proper vegetation, being clumps of godforsaken unusual grasses – proved a tripping hazard, but it was preferable to trip over a plant than a nest. Squished eggs after all were a waste of immediate food and future profit. Tussock grass lay in clumps. Most groupings of grasses were as tall as Hasselborough's kneecap, and some taller still. The wind rippled through these compact bodies of tussock in steady lines, as if the ground itself were shivering. It was as though this ancient rock was a parasite on the wider body of water, with the ocean itself shaking to dislodge it. All the while, the men on top of this crust decided to explore.

Hasselborough had no intention of staying long on this godforsaken, windswept land. His intent was to get his crew of sealers set up and to then go away to come back with more. But his curiosity possessed him. He decided to find a high point, get a sense of how big the island was, and if there was any easier point of entry for his return. Then he'd depart.

He separated the men into two groups. One to stay at their basecamp, and one to explore with him up the mountain ridges. A sailor he knew with a talent for navigation and basic cartography skills led the way. Hasselborough knew when to loosen the reins of leadership to prevent any mutinous spirit emerging from the more enterprising of the sailors and sealers. He was only going to be here a short time. Best not to be too authoritarian. It would show the men he trusted them with his island while he was gone and increase their sense of trust and security. They'd be completely fine.

He did not know his journey was being watched this time by a red eye in a twitching feathered face.

This eye had seen the future. A possible future. Experienced the horror of loved ones being melted down into oil. The sustained massacres over a century. Remembered the stickiness of blood and an ocean slicked with oil. The beaches, littered with the bones of his penguin kin and innocent seals too, ribcages picked apart for food and left behind to become bleached as driftwood. Most bodies, though, were melted down. His family, generation after generation, harvested and liquified into penguin oil.

Not this time. Not this timeline. He'd sold his soul for a chance at revenge.

Hasselborough had no idea, only the vague glimmer of profit and endless seal supplies in his eyes. He looked around. It was no Antarctica, not made of ice, but it was near barren of trees and shrub. Just this blasted tussock grass, which a man behind him twisted his ankle over and delayed the journey for another twenty minutes. Hasselborough tried to keep morale up with a jaunty sailing tune, but his voice was lost on the wind, and not even he was feeling it.

Snow was threatening to fall. Although the land was not ice, there were thick hats of snow on the higher mountain tops. Hasselborough took aim at the skua and petral cawing and hovering overhead. His shots missed, half-heated with cold. One of the birds took off with a screaming penguin chick, right from beneath the parent's protection.

'Bird and veg for dinner, d'ya reckon?' one of the men shouted. He'd crouched on one of the ridges and was examining a green plant that looked like a rhubarb cauliflower. 'Or is this a fruit?'

'Might be poisonous. You volunteering to test it for us?' Hasselborough was adventurous in all but food. Dying from eating something he shouldn't was not on his agenda.

'Mayhaps. It's all over this island. When we set up camp, I might try to boil a pot.'

'You're a braver lad than I,' Hasselborough's chortled sound was mostly lost on the breeze, even though they were shouting. 'We'll note the effects. If it's disagreeable but not deadly, it'll be supper for a while with the meat. I see not much else in the way of vegetation, and you may want to ration out what we've brought from onboard, hungry though your gullet may be.'

Fog had descended upon them, making it difficult to see much else of the party. They were but blurred smudges moving closer in the sheet of mist. A stream of breath trailed from Hasselborough's mouth. His limbs felt heavy with cold. The seals were lucky to have blubber; furs clearly were not enough. His canvas pants were thick and waterproofed, as were his boots, but the chill had seeped into his bones. It must have been approaching minus ten degrees Celsius.

He turned to the crouching man again. Mapping the layout of the island could happen with more provisions, when the mist wasn't setting in so thick. The man beside him had opened his mouth to speak, when suddenly an arc of blood and the gored beak and face of a royal penguin burst through his lips instead of words. The warm splatter shot onto Hasselborough's face, rapidly freezing into red icicles as the captain struggled to make sense of the grisly scene he was seeing. The usually white face of the bird was blackened with his comrade's blood. It opened its beak, still protruding between the slain man's lips, to let out a bloodthirsty cry more chilling than the treacherous weather.

The scream was directed right into his face. The sound was visceral, while the beak itself was coated in viscera.

The sea elephants joined the braying din, as a cacophony of birds echoed the killer's call.

On instinct, Hasselborough turned and ran down the steep hill, trying not to slip as his feet splashed through shallow puddles. The bird must have come from above. Flattened its wings and dived down the hill towards him, using its body like a feathered arrow to pierce through the man's throat and mouth.

He heard the chattering of penguins above. Saw their fuzzy outlines in the thick fog, the shadows and sounds of wings flapping as they positioned themselves on rocks. The birds had whipped themselves into a frenzy, and his heart sped up to meet their intensity. His lungs heaved. Straining heart jackhammered. His eyes widened with adrenaline, skin pinching in the sudden push against the cold. But he was frozen. The sight of the penguins was terror incarnate. One appeared to lift its beak to the sky like a wolf, but this could have just been a trick from the poor visibility. Nevertheless, a sound emerged from that moving penguin, howling like a wolf with a foghorn for a throat.

No, that was not going to be his fate! He was going to be a great man, damn it!

He ran, footfalls feeling too heavy and cumbersome on the ground as he dodged the projectile penguins throwing themselves at his back. He shouted at the smudges he had assumed were his men to run with him, only to realize they had fallen to the flightless birds. Groups of the man-eating penguins leapt onto his pitifully crying men, begging for mercy that would not come. Their wings were raised in taunting glee as they hopped from foot to foot, before they bellyflopped over the men's helpless bodies, gliding in rivers of human blood.

Hasselborough had to look away as he saw several murderous penguins making incisions through the men's flesh, ripping out entrails with beak and claw. A rockhopper penguin launched itself like a speeding bullet and grazed his ear, Hasselborough's instincts telling him to duck to the side. With the danger dodged, he looked over his shoulder to find a blood-drenched royal penguin running down the hill face after him. Its wings were raised wide as it rapidly waddled on its heinous clawed feet, beckoning Hasselborough to come in for a fight. Hasselborough had the longer legs and was creating distance, but his own feet were ill-equipped to deal with the demands of the rockface, the grip and control of his heavy boots sacrificed for insulation. His boots had been made to survive the cold.

Not the penguins. He faltered. The penguin continued to waddle. Menacingly. It had slowed down its pace, as if taunting that it had got him exactly where it wanted him. The viscera coating its beak did not stick its trap together, it let out a steady infernal trill. *Noot, noot* – it was like it was screaming at him, an extended, 'Not today. Not this time.'

Hasselborough had almost made it down the mountain when he slipped. His descent saw rocks piercing his side before he landed in pillows of fur seal. They did nothing, friendly creatures just trying to shuffle around to make him comfortable in their pile, which unfortunately made it hard for him to get purchase. He raised a hand as he tried to lift himself off their plush backs. But then the frenzied birds were upon him. His hand fell back as the cloud of black, white, and red descended.

Diprotodon

Freyja Catron

Repentance Creek, New South Wales
Tuesday afternoon

Josh came home with bones today. I watched from the veranda as he lifted them off the passenger seat and carried them into the house. It wasn't a full skeleton, just the skull and two long, curved rib bones. He carried the rib bones over his shoulder and held the skull under his arm. They looked heavy. He said he found them in the creek when he was fixing the pump, that they must've come dislodged in the floods. A crocodile, I thought. But Josh said the skull was too big and there'd never been crocodiles this far south anyway. And he was right, it *was* too big and it was different from a crocodile. It was a funny shape, its nose curved and pointed. It felt old. A bunyip, I suggested.

He showed it to Tom that night while we sat in the living room drinking. Tom balanced it on his hands and felt its weight. 'I think it's some kind of megafauna,' he said, placing it down on the arm of the sofa.

I grimaced at the skull and leant away from it into Josh. It made me feel nauseated having it in the house like that. Josh laughed at my disgust and grabbed my hand. He held it against the skull near its mouth. I imagined huge animals crawling up out of the creek toward the house. Josh's hand was hot and oily from the chips we'd been eating. I concentrated on his skin and ignored the cool smooth bone. I pulled my hand away, 'a camel skull maybe?'

'Nah,' Josh said, 'it feels old.'

The skull sat on the coffee table for days, like a vase of flowers. I didn't tell Josh, but it seemed wrong to have it there, as if taken out of some ancient time and into our living room. I asked if he'd drive to the university in town to see if they could tell what animal it came from. He wasn't interested. They wouldn't let him keep it, he said.

I went out a lot that week. I stayed at Keely's in town and took extra shifts at work. When I was home the skull was always near, in the corner of my eye while we cooked dinner, right in front of me while I watched movies on my laptop.

The skull on our coffee table dissolved the space I'd created over the past few years. Our house was bright and clean and it should have existed separate from the forest outside. When I first arrived in the valley, the bush seemed to creep into the house so that the creaking weatherboards became wind in the eucalyptus trees and small bats flew in through broken windows. But I put up posters and photos that I'd had in my room back in Brisbane, hung fairy lights above the sofa and knocked the wasp nests off the veranda railings. The lights in our house always took a long time to brighten when you switched them on, but now they seemed to take even longer and the night felt much closer.

Olary, South Australia
Friday night

Rose watched the headlights from far off bobbing like Min Min lights on the horizon. She sat on the veranda and watched for a long time. The lights were the only thing to watch with the clouds covering the stars that night and the moon almost non-existent. When the headlights were close enough she could make out a ute. A local, probably. The grey nomads all would have stopped driving for the night. The ute turned right, just before the pub, which had been closed for the past couple of weeks. 'Off-season,' Mike had said, but it was coming into school holidays now.

The ute pulled up near the site of the fire, where the road turned from tar to dirt. It sat there for a while, idling. Rose didn't recognise the car. The driver's bald head was silhouetted against the headlights. His indicator flashed, lighting up the spinifex grass by the roadside and then leaving it in darkness. It would be dangerous driving to Curnamona at that time of night. Rose wondered whether he was lost, she couldn't think of any other reason to be driving down there so late. The indicator switched off and the ute drove on. The lights receded into the low hills in the west. By then her veranda light was the only light left on in Olary. It faded out at the edge of the steps, casting the driveway in darkness. She continued to sit there though, hoping another car would pass, waiting for the road trains, waiting for the sun to rise.

Repentance Creek, New South Wales
Friday night

Josh was down at Tom's the night the ute pulled up in our driveway. The car sat by the skip, its engine running and its indicator lighting up the overgrown lantana. I didn't recognise it. Since moving to the valley I'd come to learn all the neighbours' cars so well that I could even recognise the sounds of some of their engines as they drove past. I sat on the sofa, by the megafauna bones, watching the ute's headlights reflect off the green paint on the skip. I told myself it was a lost tourist or someone looking for reception but I felt my stomach clenching uncomfortably as I stood by the window. The ute indicated right, needlessly, onto a dark empty road and drove off, toward the end of the valley. I wondered when Josh would be home. I'd tell him about the ute and he'd laugh at my fears and say that the city is much more dangerous. That's why he never wanted to live there. I looked out across the road one more time before I shut the curtains. The only lights on in the valley were the two bright ones across the creek looking like eyes in the trees. I hugged my dressing gown closer and sat by the heater in the kitchen, away from the skull. It was finally starting to feel like winter.

Olary, South Australia

Saturday morning

Rose watched the sun rise over the salmon-coloured earth. Even after being back so long, the winters still shocked her. In the winter, the light had a glaring, pale kind of brightness that made it hard to see. A cold wind blew up through the stunted eucalyptus trees and across Rose's face. She thought for a moment of a time long ago, cycling to class, watching the winter sun rise over dark suburban streets, the handlebars icy beneath her fingers.

After the fire, she'd considered returning to Adelaide, but now even the thought that her old suburb still existed shocked her. She'd become one of those people from her hometown that she'd hated so much when she was younger, so afraid to leave. She kept telling herself she'd go away, even for a weekend, but she didn't. She couldn't.

It was dark inside, after the morning sun, and the linoleum tiles stuck to her socks. A freight train creaked as it slowed to a stop across the road. She made toast and opened a newspaper she'd picked up at the roadhouse last week. She would walk over to Mike's and use his Wi-Fi later. She'd see if her sister wanted to Skype and maybe she'd apply for some jobs in Broken Hill. Outside the train started up again, heading for Adelaide.

Repentance Creek, New South Wales
Saturday morning

Josh came home late and snored like he'd
been drinking. He was still asleep when I woke
up the next morning. It was early, and I laid
there for a while, listening to his breath. The
wind was blowing at the palm trees in the front
yard and their little round seeds clattered on the
corrugated iron roof. I climbed over Josh and
went out into the living room. It looked like it
would rain again today. The clouds came in from
the coast, up over Goonengerry. At the other
end of the valley the air was hazy, and rain was
already beginning to fall. I'd have to be quick if I
wanted to stay dry. I picked up the bones on the
coffee table and wrapped them in my jumper.
The skull was heavy and where it was exposed it
was cold and almost slimy.

I walked fast through the paddock to the
creek, hoping to avoid the rain. The path was
steep above the deep pools, the plunge pools, we

call them. Josh told me that they were formed by lava millions of years ago. That was why the rocks looked almost liquid. And why the small pools – more like rock pools than swimming holes – were so deep. He said that he used to be able to dive down and touch the bottom when he was a kid but that it hurt his ears too much now. I never really believed him about that, I hadn't even gotten close to the bottom.

I stood by the edge of the biggest pool and unwrapped the skull, placing the rib bones on the rocks beside me. I pushed the bones in with my feet and held the skull out above the dark water. Its splash was louder than I expected, more solid. For a moment it seemed to silence the frogs and the rush of the creek further downstream. Rain began to fall where the creek widened and soon it fell on me too. I shook out my jumper and wrapped it around my shoulders.

Olary, South Australia
Saturday afternoon

Across the road, some tourists parked their campervan near where Julie's house used to be. They wandered over to the site of the fire, peering through broken glass and piles of scrap metal. Rose hadn't been back to the site in over a year but watching the tourists she felt a little of their morbid curiosity for the first time.

Rose found it hard to picture Julie's old place when she looked through the fence at the rubble. The piles of blackened corrugated iron and wire seemed very distant from the sheds and chicken coops that once filled Julie's backyard. She stepped over the remnants of the barbed wire fence, past the stone chimney that had survived where the newer buildings hadn't.

There was a circle of stones behind the rubble of Julie's shack. They were the old sandstone type that historical buildings are made of. Rose had never noticed the well before, it would have been covered before the fire. The stones were old but there was a metal ladder attached to the inner wall. Rose picked up a chunk of brick and dropped it into the well then waited for, but hardly expected, a splash. There was a thud on dry earth far below.

For a while she stared down the well, hypnotised by its blackness. The ladder looked new enough and strong. Rose crouched down and shook it with her hand to test it. It held tight to the stones. She felt around in her jacket pocket, past old receipts and hair ties. She didn't use her phone much, but she was glad to find it there. She turned on the torch and shone down the well, lighting up the first few rungs of the ladder. The cold air on her face made her think of a cave by the ocean.

She tested the ladder once more and began to descend. Very quickly the bright desert sunlight faded and the sounds from above ground were muted. In the well, it was much colder and she expected dampness and moss on the walls but the stones were as dry as the rest of Olary. The darkness reminded Rose of the desert at night, when you can't tell whether the space around you is small or endless. She'd gone down only a dozen or so rungs before she began to climb back out of the well, toward the circle of blue above. She didn't like how the dark felt down there, less like a cave by the ocean than like a tunnel or the end of the world. She went to move her phone to her mouth so she could grip the ladder tighter. The metal was cold on her hands and the dry air was hard to breathe. It tasted stale, like air that hadn't been breathed in a long time. The phone slipped and clattered downward, the torchlight catching the rungs of the ladder as it fell. The sound of it landing on the ground far below came as a solid clunk and the well was dark again.

Somehow it was less frightening to be descending with a purpose even without light. She moved quickly and kept her eyes straight ahead – looking up at the sky disoriented her. Soon, instead of another rung below her foot, she felt the ground. The earth was dry and sandy, like an ephemeral river bed. She wondered when this well was last full of water. She wondered whether groundwater slipped silently below her feet still.

Above her, the circle of sky looked two-dimensional. She crouched down in the sand and felt around for her phone. Instead, she felt something cool and damp and smooth. Next to it, she found her phone, screen cracked but its torch still shining onto the dirt. As she picked it up, it shone across the ground and over the other object she'd felt. Sickened, Rose thought she saw a human skeleton below her and a thousand outback horror stories passed through her mind. But the skeleton wasn't human and it wasn't a full skeleton at all. Just a large skull and some ribs. A cow maybe, but it was too big by far. It was hard to tell by the torch light. She took off her jacket and tied it around the bones, slinging it over her shoulder as she began to climb back out of the well.

This time she looked up at the sky while she climbed willing it closer. It wasn't getting closer though, and despite each step she took, she seemed to remain in the same place. The heavy bones were pulling on her, keeping her slow. But then the light hit her eyes and the desert air stung her throat. She sat on the edge of the well for a moment. She wanted badly to be back at her house sitting on the veranda. She could relax out of the fire site and away from the well.

The pub had opened and a car was parked up outside. She could smell food frying. Rose sat on the steps leading up to her house and unwrapped the bones. They were a little slimy, and still inexplicably damp. The skull had a strange shape, it was too big for a cow and its nose was beak-like. She carried it inside and placed it on the kitchen table, as a centrepiece.

The Thing with Teeth

Maz Howard

I come back to the human part on the way home. My skin regrows over torn up flesh and sticks to the nylon passenger seat, a mixture of sweat and blood. We are somewhere on the road, somewhere between the forest and our home. Abacus is behind the wheel, Fletcher in the back, and the radio is on even though we're not close enough to Adelaide for it to be more than static yet. In the passenger seat, I am still newborn flesh.

Fletcher drapes someone's jacket over me from the backseat – I am not steady enough in my bones to figure out if it's mine or not.

Something might be broken. Something is almost always broken so this is hardly an ingenious prediction. The something in this case might be a rib which makes me wish, for one wild moment, that we were still in the forest. This kind of break hurts less under the moonlight.

By the time my throat has started to fit inside my human neck, the radio is playing something that I still can't make out and Fletcher is snoring in the backseat. There is something thick and coarse matting the back of my tongue, but I am not brave enough to cough it away just yet. My chest is still tight enough that anything more violent than a shallow breath is bound to ache. Spewing hairballs out the window of a moving car is never fun anyway.

Instead, I ignore the weight of it in my mouth and say, 'Did I *kill* something?'

My voice – this early into the human part – is always half-rasp, half-whisper. I know only Abacus will hear it. She shrugs, keeps her eyes on the dark road, and lifts one hand from the steering wheel to turn the radio up just slightly, which is the same thing as saying yes.

'What was it?' I ask, a little louder. The tangled weight in my throat tickles the roof of my mouth when I talk. It is beginning to feel more and more like some variety of fur. I try to focus on something else but my brain, still only halfway human, is mostly one-track.

'A possum. It wasn't worse than usual,' Abacus says, except in a way that makes it sound like it was.

I frown at a piece of fluff caught in the latch of the glove compartment. I want to pick it out, but my arm feels heavier than I'm used to, like something leaden attached at the wrong angle to my shoulder.

'I don't remember.'

Memory fatigue is one of the more famed side effects of a transformation, but I've almost mastered my control at this point. I only miss flashes now, like I'll remember tensing the muscles in my legs to jump and I'll remember the twigs crackling when my paws crash back into the earth, but the moment in the air will be gone. I might have forgotten the snap of the possum's spine, but I should remember the shape of its flesh between my teeth.

'We only lost you for a minute.'

Abacus takes a right turn and uses it to avoid facing me, as though her words will fly out the driver's side window and leave no impact.

'A *minute?*'

She sighs. The headlights glint off a cat's eye and illuminate the flare of her nostrils for a moment.

'A half hour tops,' she says. 'You were lucid almost the whole night.'

Half an hour is too long to lose control of your limbs. Half an hour is enough time to catch, kill, and consume a possum. Or God knows what else that Abacus is refusing to tell me about.

Because I am angry and anger is the most effective form of adrenaline, I lift my arm and pick the fluff from the glove compartment. Something clicks painfully in my thorax, but the action settles my skin, letting the human sneak a little further in.

'Do you know what happened to my ribs?' I ask, instead of letting the anger curl my tongue. When you are half monster hidden under human flesh, you get a lot of practice at compartmentalising.

'Why? What's wrong with your ribs?'

I catch Abacus glancing over at me, one cheek dimpled between her teeth, but she looks back at the road before I can do anything to exchange the concern for a smile.

'Something's broken on the right.'

I stare out the windscreen as well. The dawn is beginning to break but fog hangs in patches above the tarmac, washing out the suburban buildings on either side. I don't recognise this street, although my senses are still too feral to be trustworthy. I would crack the window and test the air for the smell of Fletcher's house if I wasn't still working the beast out of my system.

'Fletcher will set it at home,' I say because Abacus' tense silence is far louder than her voice had been. She doesn't respond which is how I know the broken rib has something to do with the possum I don't remember eating.

When we pull into the carpark underneath Fletcher's apartment block, the familiar ache has settled itself around my bones. The ache is my favourite part. Every full moon lasts three days; the transformation itself passes mostly in a blur. It's the day after that hurts the most, when my bones reknit and I bleed through bandages by the hour, but the pain of becoming human again will never be as bad as feeling sanity slip steadily from my control as the moon rises.

The three of us have the journey from the front door to Fletcher's bedroom down to a science. Abacus leads the way and I walk right behind her, because hers is the most familiar scent my animalistic brain will cling to. Fletcher brings up the rear, because she's the only person in the world I would trust to catch me if I collapsed.

The first few moons after our parents kicked Abacus and me out, we would knock into too many doorframes or forget to remove our shoes and Fletcher's dad's silhouette would loom down the hallway, confused and disgruntled at being woken. But we are old hands at this now. I barely notice we've started walking before Fletcher is helping me lie on the floor, one of her hands cupped over the right side of my chest. I twist my head sideways until I can rub my cheek against the shaggy rug. There is an itch behind my jaw, after the moon, as my teeth reacquaint themselves with my gums.

Things go wrong like this: Fletcher ices my chest until it is numb and because the nerves in my left arm have not worked as nerves are supposed to since I was bitten, I cannot feel much of anything between my waist and my neck; she leaves to get breakfast, because she's always hungry and because I always need a moment alone with my sister after a moon; I try to sit upright, which seems like a solid idea because I cannot feel much of anything between my waist and my neck, but turns out to be my most painful idea of the night; and because I am in pain and no one else is in the room, Abacus cries.

The spasm in my chest is enough to shock my human brain into catching up with its human senses and I finally notice there is a chunk of hair missing at the side of Abacus' head.

'Who did that?' is the first thing I ask which, in retrospect, is a foolish question, but my brain during moons knows only *protect pack* and *kill possum.* Abacus squirms and rubs two fingers over her semi-bald patch and does not reply.

My chest is already mostly on fire from the effort of sitting up and my sister is frowning like she has a lie forming on her tongue, so I cough. It feels like snapping each of my ribs by hand, but the thick knot unsticks from my throat, and I spit it into a tissue. It is shapeless and drenched with saliva, impossible to discern where it came from, but somehow it solidifies what I already know.

'I tried to bite you,' I say.

'I broke your ribs,' Abacus says, which is not really a response and certainly isn't a fair exchange. 'Eye for an eye.'

I want to tell her that's not what that means, that a broken rib heals and someone like me never truly finds their way back to their humanity, but the door creaks open and the smell of warm bread and eggs wafts inside.

Fletcher makes me lie down again and by the time she and Abacus have finished eating, I am slipping in and out of consciousness. They settle around me, the three of us lined up with shoulders and elbows brushing. We are pack animals, and the full moon never permits them to be very far from me. Most of the way asleep and still half-formed around weak muscles, I feel Abacus wind her fingers through my hair. It means *I'm sorry*. It means *I forgive you*. It means *I am here and that's all*.

I wish sometimes, in flashes of bitterness between the trees or in the car or on the floor of Fletcher's bedroom, that I had bled out after the bite, or maybe that I had not been brave enough to go looking for trouble.

Or maybe that I had never heard of werewolves at all.

This is how it works: everyone thinks they are too human to be a monster; everyone thinks they are the exception; everyone closes their eyes before they dream (except me).

Lycanthropy is very similar to running a fever when you are six years old. Your body is made mostly of thermal energy during transformation and when you come back to yourself, everything is hazy and torpid, and it feels like seeing the ceiling above your bed for the first time. The difference is, when you wake from a fever dream, your mother's cool hands are never more than a room away. When you return from a full moon, all your bones are broken, and your teeth don't fit in your mouth.

The worst thing about coming back is that I can always remember when the human part was the only shape my body knew and this skin was just skin, begging to be torn. I might not recall the possums I kill between my teeth, but the version of me that saw nothing but humanity in a scraped-up knee is locked inside my head forever.

This is how it works: twenty-two-year-old university dropout gives up her lifelong dream of veterinary science to chase a rumour through the outback; twenty-two-year-old university dropout climbs mountains without a guide because *she* is the exception, *she* is too human to be a monster; twenty-two-year-old university dropout loses half the flesh around her shoulder, the mobility in her left arm, and the respect of most of her peers in one fell swoop.

You can never prepare for the worst because the worst is always the thing you never thought could happen to you, until you are bleeding into a patch of spinifex halfway up a mountain in the Flinders Ranges.

But after the worst thing happens – after you survive the werewolf attack, after the moon shreds you, limb from limb – you come back. You wash your ribs in the bathroom sink of your best friend's house and you pop each finger back into its socket and you wake up (in the passenger seat or on the carpeted floor) with someone's hand in your hair. And that's all there is.

The Garden House: A Gothic Story

Patrick Taylor

There is a structure in the grounds which eludes the attention of my parents' tours of their historic estate. While they promise guests a detailed overview of the surrounds – the natural and architectural beauty of which they take great pride in – visitors are never permitted to roam freely in the garden. Beyond the arbours and gated rosebushes, yet still on the lay of the general land, lies an old wooden long house, hidden by rows of wilder green, the building itself smothered in vines as though it were as old as the dark grey trees around it.

The long house is a rare thing: a building with its own sound. Mills, of course, have the grinding of stone and the creaking of wood in motion. Barns have the muffled chatter and braying of animals in sodden pens.

The long house has the buzzing of flies.

All day and into the night, a constant, repugnant hum sneaks into our ears from the edge of the garden, never sleeping or slowing. Sitting in the hollow metal garden chairs by the violets, if you tune your senses away from the other sounds of the outdoors, you will hear it. You cannot help but hear it.

My parents took to lying and told their guests all they heard was bees, hard at their pleasant work. In fact, this fiction had begun well before I first encountered the long house. Not knowing any better, I accepted this as truth, never questioning it even in the coldest winters when the dry, dying flowers were barren of pollinators and the hum persisted regardless.

I clearly recall when I finally investigated the absence of the bees. It was a late morning, in the earliest days of my remaining childhood memories, when I detected that high, constant tone more distinctly than usual in the outdoor air. Curious, as all children are for a part of their formative years, I investigated the flowerbeds for the reputed culprits, inexplicably enthusiastic to see them among the petals. The remaining flowers were interspersed only with orange leaves that fell from above; it was autumn, and there was not a bee to be found, certainly not in the great numbers suggested by the faint but forceful sounds around the garden.

Surprised and disappointed by the passage of seasons, I explored further, towards the vague rim that contained the more cultivated greenery of the garden, my mind now fiercely attuned to the sound. The drone was ever constant, though it changed in perceived volume as I routinely lost and rediscovered its direction. I paid no heed to the fact that it was leading me further away from the lavender and bougainvillaea, the sweet scent substituted first for the plainness of dirt and leaf litter, then slowly by something else, damp and ammonic.

The trimmed grass gave way to wilder patches, forgotten or ignored. As I trudged on under rusted iron arches and meagre fencing half sunk into the dust, all of which were choked by nameless species of vine, the grass itself dissipated. In its place was shoe-deep mud, still glistening from the morning dew and much more hostile to my progress than the previous garden paths.

However, the buzzing in my ears had undeniably grown. My childish enthusiasm to see *something*, merely for the sake of seeing it, willed me forward.

The manicured grace of the garden had been lost entirely by this point. Though I was still flanked with green and earthy colours, they now belonged to wild, towering bushes; stubbornly gnarled trees of the woods; and layers of thorny vines that cloaked every surface like countless brides' veils. This was unlike anything I had contended with before. The garden I had left behind was akin to a well-ordered house: each route through the former corridors had been marked by hedges and blossoms; each was predictable from the first step, one's destination always within sight. Now, the random paths I found through this wilderness had more in common with a spelunker's descent into a cave – nature closing in from every angle, killing the increasingly dim light – as I was invited by necessity down tunnels and chasms that led everywhere and nowhere, without promise of a safe return.

Without reason, abandoned by the careful architecture of those who tended the garden in my and my family's interest, I was led on only by that persistent buzzing. I focused so deeply upon it that it seemed to emanate from inside my own skull, becoming a sense in its own right to guide me to a single objective – although I did not yet know what that object was.

Just as I began to lose faith in the unseen call, I came across the last thing I expected to see: a long house.

It took some time to realise the strangeness of this new arrival in my surroundings. I accepted its presence well before the more reasonable response – to question who built this place, to whom it belonged and for what reason I had never seen it before – emerged in my mind. Perhaps this lapse of thought was due to the dark, knotted wood that the imposing shack had been roughly constructed from, giving the impression that it was an incidental part of the natural, untended world I had entered. The small building's disordered, simple structure and the vines and branches that crept up it resembled a gnarled copse which had all fallen in the same spot, rather than a house erected by human hands.

Then again, perhaps my unquestioning approach towards the dark hut was due to the buzzing in the air which began to reach the height of its crescendo. The endless cacophony both deadened my senses to reason and suggested to my childish mind that I had finally discovered the object of my curiosity.

Thus, I moved forward, the deafening hum of flies beating at my ears. I clearly remember, though I do not know why, that my hands were outstretched as I walked, reaching outwards towards the blackened long house as though eagerly anticipating a new toy to experiment with.

There were three glass windows on the long side of the building and a windowless door on the short side. The door was likely bolted, but I did not think to investigate it at the time. Instead, my meandering curiosity led me straight to the middle window. It is a child's first wish upon seeing a closed door to find out what lies behind it; this took precedence, thankfully, over actually entering the unknown place.

My outstretched hands met with a window slick with grime. After prying away a few wayward strands of vine which I thought would impede my view, I rubbed at the glass. The accumulation of years of dirt came off on my hand, painting the skin dark. The glass underneath, aside from feeling strangely more brittle and older than the windows of my family home, was also warm to the touch. An unexplained heat seemed to radiate from within the building as though from a source found deeper inside this wood and glass enclosure. The heat of the surface called to mind the sensation of touching a glass lamp after the flame inside has been extinguished and the warm gases idle within.

As I continued to remove the grime, and my hands became progressively filthier, my curiosity was frustrated by what first seemed to be a deeper stain, too stubborn to remove. My view of the inside of the house remained obscured in inky darkness. Wiping more forcefully at the window – to the point I feared I may break through its brittleness entirely – I came to realise that this next curtain of filth lay on the inner side of the window. I rubbed the dirt from my palms onto my trousers and resigned myself to pressing my face against the glass, hoping that my eyes would adjust enough to detect something beyond the obstruction. I continued to stare patiently while the endless screaming of the flies urged me on.

My patience yielded a grim reward. The first realisation gleaned from my insistent stare was that the inner layer of grime was not what it seemed. Beyond the window was a black pattern of constant, shifting motion. Specks of nothingness flitted rapidly past my vision, never still enough that my eyes could track just one. There were thousands, it seemed, of dark spots before me at a time. They created an additional barrier to my sight, an incessant field of black noise in the darkness – created by an enormous swarm of flies, trapped just behind the window.

In time, my eyes grew used to this, too. I learned automatically to see beyond the secondary coat of shifting blackness, and through it I could have my first clear view of the inside. The walls were unpainted and unadorned; the same harsh, dark wood of the outside, which I had feared would splinter my hands, appeared inside of the room. The floor, at least, had a few hastily laid floorboards; it would not have surprised me to see a mere dirt floor between the walls.

The room, as far as my strained eyes could tell, was empty but for one thing. As I stared more intently to confirm that the visual confusion had not misled me, the sight arrested my full attention.

There were three figures, human figures, slumped against the far wall.

Instantly, I felt the cold grip of terror, its frozen hands pressing into my back. It was the same sense of utter dread, that near-paralysis and lack of action, which I had only felt in my most unbearable nightmares.

Unable to remove myself from the window, I numbly realised that all three bodies were unclothed; that their bare skin, like their long, matted hair, was unwashed and covered in specks of dirt; and that flies swarmed and landed on the arms, legs and torsos, then flew once more; perhaps taking succour from their grotesquely bloodless skin; perhaps simply resting their wings before recommencing their flight.

As foul as the sight was, its unexpected detestability was not the cause of my terror.

My mind's sole concern was that, until this very moment, I had assumed I was alone in this abandoned, buzzing place. I had taken for granted that I would be able to observe this unfamiliar world freely without being observed myself. That enticing possibility, all the stronger for my childish curiosity, called me forward just as strongly as the flies. Here the promise threatened to be abruptly broken, my security stolen by these collapsed strangers. 'Perhaps they heard my approach,' said a thought that trickled like ice water from the back of my mind down my spine. 'Perhaps there are more of them, just out of sight, buried from view by the endless flies.'

It was at that moment, as though hearing the voice at the back of my mind, that the body in the centre of my vision raised its head and looked at me.

I did not move. I could do nothing but stare back. Yet, for all my staring and for all the clarity with which I can recall the rest of that day, I still struggle to summon to mind the face of the wretched sufferer who lifted their head. Any attempt to do so conjures a blank space framed by matted, weedy hair. And yet, the sensation of being seen, of my actions and expressions being captured in another's eyes, lingers more clearly in this memory than the stranger's face.

That is the last that I recall before a pair of hands snatched me away from the window.

The vision before me had been so absorbing and the sound of flies so deafening that I had failed to notice my mother's approach from some distance behind. My paralysis at the window clearly gave her more than enough time to guess at the direction in which I had stumbled and to follow the path to where I stood. She pulled me hard – harder than I thought her capable of, as though she were trying to remove a stump from the earth – and, hoisting my little body in her arms, carried me away from the dark long house.

The audacity of this intervention caused me to somehow forget my prior terror. I protested loudly and rambunctiously as she led me back through the wild path I had trod for her, the long house falling from present terror into dreamlike memory the moment we turned away from it. By the time I could finally wrench my head around and survey the way we had come, the hut was gone, hidden away by trees, vines and distance. Only the coarse patches of dirt caked on my trousers could persuade me that it had existed at all, that my mother did not merely wake me from a nightmare.

It was the same dirt as our own garden, I realised; the same soil that nurtured the lavender my mother plucked and placed on my pillow, the true source of the smells and sights of home. The nightmare was inextricably tied to our property, so close that it might have sprouted from the same bush, might have been a petal on the same bloom.

I asked many questions through my mother's admonishments and my own tears. Most of them began with the same word: *why*? Why were these people in our garden? Why were they suffering? Why had I never seen them before and why weren't we helping them?

Her answer to my final question I remember clearer than the remainder of that day. I have found myself repeating it often, even at my current age. It is a balm for the dirty, frightened child who, ever more rarely, emerges in my heart, his expression of frozen terror now a distant memory, a vivid memory, certainly, but merely a historical account of a past I happened to live. My memory of his fear is as objective and impassive as a photograph in my hand, as though I had never felt it at all. She said: 'They must go *somewhere*.'

So, the answer remains the same today. It was the first and only time I visited the long house, but I know it has not changed, and the grim duty for which it was built does not concern me. It is merely a necessity, the particulars of which I do not need to know, save that they would not be different wherever it happened to be built. The flowers have their beds; the vines, their arbours; us, our fine home; and the flies, and their fellow residents, the long house.

Violets

Svetlana Sterlin

Here the leaves don't fall. Nothing blooms in spring except for the weeds that find their way through the cracks of Gumdale's sun-bleached driveways. Violet once heard that's how the light gets in – through the cracks.

Here the seasons have a way of interweaving. Violet has the windows down so she can feel the wind through her hair as she drives. Has autumn arrived so soon?

Here nobody pays attention to the speed limits, but Violet has never received a speeding ticket. She smiles as she thinks about Vincent on a plane on his way back to her, about how excited their daughters must be to see him after school, about Charlie wagging his tail at the front door.

Violet is still smiling as she steers her sleek family SUV onto Baxter Road, not noticing the blanket of quiet that subdues even the trees. The wispiest of breezes skims her bare face. She nuzzles up against it as the road unfurls before her. Here the asphalt meanders like a river.

Violet is still smiling when she glides to a stop beside a small, cardboard-coloured car at a traffic light. She looks over and nods at the driver, a woman of about the same age. She returns the gesture. For a moment, Violet thinks that maybe they know each other, but the woman turns back to face the road, and Violet can't be sure.

The light turns green just as Violet's phone *ping*s. She glances down to see a text from Vincent. Beside her, the brown car pulls away. Violet tells herself she'll reply to Vincent as soon as she can.

She drives, smiling again as the woods fall away to offer a sweeping view of the last remaining farm in Gumdale. She doesn't think about how those fields will soon be fenced off and dug up and turned into another housing development – developed, in fact, by the same company responsible for Woodlands, the home she's driving to now.

The farm is obscured by the neat forest that tells Violet she's almost home.

She's still smiling when a new car appears further down the road – a ute, careering straight towards her and the brown car ahead. Violet doesn't understand what she's looking at, doesn't understand that the driver is on the wrong side of the road, that the driver has no control of their vehicle.

The brown car's taillights glare red. Violet takes her foot off the accelerator, her smile like an awkwardly hung painting on the frame of her face.

She coasts along Baxter Road as the approaching ute gathers speed and swerves with a loud squeal. Only now does Violet steer her SUV to the side of the road and slam on the brakes.

The other woman's car veers to the left. At this moment, Violet remembers the horse she grew up with on a farm not far from the one she just passed. She watches the little brown car nudge against the light pole as gentle as her horse used to nudge a bale of hay.

The ute skids past her, whirls around and zooms back to wherever it came from.

Violet sits, not moving, not even blinking.

The static silence of Baxter Road settles back into place like a record on a phonograph.

Violet kills the engine, stumbles out of her SUV and trots hesitantly towards the brown car as if she thinks it might blow up. It doesn't.

She peers at the woman clenching the steering wheel. Violet taps on the window. The woman is startled and breaks into a smile. Violet smiles, too. Again, she feels like she knows the woman.

'Hello,' Violet says.

The woman rolls her window down.

'Are you alright?' Violet asks, eyeing the car and the woman's body, though she doesn't appear to be injured.

'Oh, yes, I'm totally fine! Are you?'

'Me? Yeah, he just – gosh, he just came out of nowhere, didn't he?' Violet laughs. 'Um – should we call the police?'

The woman blinks.

'I mean – I'm not sure,' Violet says. 'You know, what's the procedure in these situations?'

The woman doesn't answer.

'Are you sure you're alright?' Violet asks. 'You're not hurt anywhere, are you?'

The woman doesn't move. Violet opens the door, wincing, but the woman doesn't react. Violet reaches in to feel along the woman's arms, neck, sides. She looks at Violet, and something about the way she turns her head reminds her of her daughters when she tucks them in to bed.

'What's your name? You can hear me, can't you?'

Violet spots a handbag on the passenger seat. She reaches across the woman and pulls the bag towards herself. She fishes out a wallet, flips it open and sees her own name printed on the driver's license inside. She looks up at the other Violet.

'Your name is Violet? My name's Violet, too.'

The two women look at each other and laugh.

'Hi, Violet,' says Violet.

'Hi,' says the Other Violet. Her body relaxes as she turns towards Violet.

Violet laughs and gives the woman her handbag. 'I think I should sit with you for a bit. Just to make sure you're alright.'

Violet walks around to the passenger side. She pauses to assess the damage to the front of the car – a small dent matching the one on the metal light pole, but nothing major.

She slides onto the passenger seat and closes the door. The car is silent. Violet glances around and notices that the windows are already up again.

She shifts in her seat and clears her throat. 'So, do you think we should call the police? I don't really know what to do in these situations.'

The Other Violet stares straight ahead. 'I don't think that's – oh.'

'What? What is it?'

'I forgot to buy carrots. I've just been at the shops.'

Violet turns to her. 'Really? So have I.'

Violet settles back into her seat. Every sound is audible in the compact cabin. Violet shifts and glances into the rear-view mirror. The road is empty.

'Are you sure you're alright?' Violet asks again.

'Um – I don't know. I don't feel anything.'

'Maybe I should call an ambulance. Just in case.' Violet reaches into her pocket. 'Oh, I left my phone in my car. Can I borrow yours?'

When the Other Violet doesn't answer, Violet reaches for the phone in the console, takes the Other Violet's hand and presses her thumb to the touchpad. She dials 000 and watches the rise and fall of the Other Violet's chest quicken as she waits for the operator.

'Yes, hello, my name is Violet O'Connor. I'm here with another woman. We've just – she's just been in an accident. Nothing severe, but there was a slight impact.' Violet lowers her voice. 'She was a little unresponsive at first. I think she's in shock. We're pulled over on the side of Baxter Road near the Woodlands housing development in Gumdale. Okay, thank you.' Violet hangs up and turns to the Other Violet. 'Do you have anyone I should call?'

'I guess … my husband. Vincent.'

Violet stills. 'Vincent?'

'Victor.'

Violet blinks. 'Oh, right. Victor.'

She scrolls through Violet's contacts and finds Victor's profile. She dials the number.

'But he won't like that,' the Other Violet says. 'He's at work. I wouldn't want to disturb him.'

'What? You've been in an accident! I'm sure he won't mind.'

The Other Violet reaches out and grabs Violet's wrist. Violet drops the phone into her lap.

'Please. Don't.'

They both look down at the screen, at Victor's name spelled out above the dial pad.

'It's okay,' Violet says. 'I can do the talking.'

The Other Violet curls over, pressing her head to her knees, and begins to sob.

'What is it?' Violet asks.

'I'm going to die.'

'What? No, you're not!'

The call goes to voicemail and the Other Violet shudders, sitting up. But Violet twists in her seat as she hears a faint ringing from behind – from her own car, her own phone. She looks back down at the Other Violet's phone then up at the Other Violet.

'What are you – what's going on?'

'Please help me,' the Other Violet says.

Violet takes the Other Violet's face in her hands. 'Stop it. Stop it now.'

The Other Violet trembles under Violet's palms. 'I'm going to die.'

Violet lets go of her face. 'You're not even hurt.'

The Other Violet cowers. 'Can you just – tell me something. Please. Tell me about you.'

Violet stares. She softens back into her seat, remembering who she is, and folds her arms across her lap. 'I – there's nothing. There's nothing to tell.'

'But you have to have a story.'

'Well, I –' Violet starts then stops. 'I don't have a story. I have a husband. And three daughters. And a dog, Charlie.' Violet smiles.

'No, tell me about *you*.'

Violet takes the Other Violet's hand and glances in the rear-view mirror. 'Just hang on. You'll be fine.'

Violet watches a breeze comb through the trees outside. The road is still empty.

Violet swallows. 'Gosh, I love it here. Don't you? Where do you live, exactly?'

'Behind the Woodlands development.'

'Oh, I live inside it. You know, one of those cul-de-sacs. It's actually quite nice.'

'I bet.'

'So, what do you do? Do you have kids?'

'No. Well, I did. I mean, I do. But they're not mine anymore.'

'Oh. Well, what's your husband like?'

'What do *you* do?'

Violet shifts. 'Well, I guess I stay home most days. Cleaning, cooking. Taking care of Charlie. You know – I'm a mum.'

'Is that what you wanted to be when you grew up?'

Violet swallows a laugh, almost chokes on it. 'No, I guess not. I wanted to be – well, it's silly. I wanted to be a dancer.' She drops the Other Violet's hand and turns to look out the window.

'That's not silly. You could still do it.'

Violet's laughter crawls back up her throat. 'Gosh, no. It's far too late now. I guess I could be a dance teacher if I wanted to. But now I don't know what I want.'

The Other Violet's phone rings. Violet looks down at the screen. The caller ID says 'Victor'. Her hand finds the Other Violet's arm.

'Look, Violet,' Violet says, then twists around in her seat as another sound draws her attention. Sirens.

'Violet, look! You're going to be alright.'

The ambulance pulls up behind Violet's car. She turns back to the Other Violet, but her eyes have glazed over. She's dead.

***

Two young women climb out of the ambulance and move towards the Violets like they're flowing to the rhythm of a well-rehearsed dance. One paramedic carries a first-aid kit. The other clears her throat, prepares to address the Violets. But at the window of the cardboard-coloured car, she stops short, and the other paramedic does, too.

Violet knows they must be outside now. She doesn't hear them through the closed windows, but she knows they must be close.

'Could you please step out of the vehicle, ma'am?'

'Ma'am?'

'Yes, could you please step out of the vehicle?'

Violet blinks and extracts her fingers from the Other Violet's. She steps out of the car while the paramedic leans over the Other Violet and unpacks her kit.

The autumn breeze pauses to allow Violet to walk back to her car. Loose gravel shifts under her shoes. She doesn't notice herself trip.

***

Violet doesn't hear her daughters' chatter on the way home from school. She has already asked them how their day was, and as usual the conversation has curved away from her.

'Mum?'

Violet shakes the static away. 'What did you say?' She glances in the rear-view at Harriet, her eldest.

She understands now, almost remembers, how her own mother must have felt – building a life in a new country, married to a white man. Violet recalls sitting in the back seat on the way home from school, catching her mother's eye in the rear-view mirror. When she was older, she sat

beside her up front. Those quiet car rides made
Violet want more than one child of her own.

'I asked how your day was,' Harriet says.

'Oh. It was – you know. I did the groceries.'

'Is that all?'

Violet glances at Harriet in the mirror.

'Well, no. Something happened today.'

Grace and Nina look up. Violet shifts in her
seat.

'I was driving back from the shops when
this…' Violet pauses, swallows. 'This car just
came out of nowhere, speeding down the
wrong side of the road.' Violet turns onto
Valencia Street. 'And there was another woman.
In another car. And she swerved to avoid this
oncoming ute. And she hit a pole.' Violet turns
onto Azalea Avenue. 'But she wasn't hurt. I
went over and sat with her and held her hand.
And we laughed over the fact that her name was
Violet, too. And then she – she passed away.
Right there. Holding my hand. I think it was

shock.' Violet sniffles. 'She had a husband. And kids. Well, sort of. I mean, she wanted kids. I'm sure she did.' Violet bites her lip.

Nina and Grace exchange a look. They don't speak.

Violet turns onto Baxter Road.

Harriet looks around as if she might find the right words on the passenger seat. 'Oh, gosh, Mum. I'm so sorry.'

Violet straightens and wipes her nose with the sleeve of her jumper. 'It was – it was right there, actually.' She nods out the window.

The girls twist around in the back seat. All they see is a slightly dented light pole, brown grass and loose gravel on the side of the road, as if nothing much had ever happened there.

Violet clears her throat. 'Dad's home,' she says.

'Really?' Grace asks, forgetting the pole.

Harriet elbows her. 'Did you tell him about it?' she asks.

'No, I... haven't spoken to him yet.'

'Will you? Tell him, I mean.'

'Oh, I don't know. He's got enough on his mind.'

***

Violet pulls the car into her cul-de-sac. The houses in Woodlands all look the same. The hedges are trimmed and not a single stray leaf litters the lawns. Trees stand sentinel beside each driveway.

Nina, Grace and Harriet pile out of the car and stumble over each other to wrestle their schoolbags out of the boot.

Violet stays in the car and watches her daughters ascend the steps. Halfway up, the door opens. Vincent stands on the threshold. The girls throw themselves into his open arms.

Violet keeps her hands on the wheel. Her foot teeters above the accelerator, though the engine is off. She wonders what Vincent would do if she let their SUV roll down the driveway, out onto the cul-de-sac, back onto the main thoroughfare, all the way to Baxter Road and someplace she hasn't thought of before.

Vincent raises his eyes to her. She lets go of the wheel, climbs out of the car and walks towards him. She walks so slowly that their daughters have let go of him and gone inside by the time she's at the bottom of the steps. She walks so slowly that she has time to memorise Vincent's new face – the fresh stubble, the shadowed whites of his eyes, the sagging skin.

'Hey,' he says.

'Hi.'

They put their arms around each other and stay on the top step for a long time.

'I missed you,' Vincent says.

Violet pulls away. 'I have to get the groceries.'

'Oh. Okay. Well, I'm knackered.'

Violet looks at him then turns away. She's going to let it go but then she pauses. 'You know, this isn't …'

'What?'

'Never mind.'

She offers a waning smile and goes down to the car. By the time she's started unloading the groceries, Vincent has left the doorway. The street becomes quiet. Violet looks towards the gaping front door at the looming rectangular shadow in its place.

She carries the groceries up to the house, taking three trips there and back. She emerges once more, empty-handed, and surveys the sunset falling over her suburb.

'No, this isn't,' she says, though Vincent isn't around to hear.

***

Here the mornings are bright. Sunlight slants down over the orange-speckled lawn. It's scraggy and unevenly trimmed, and it's the middle of spring. Here the houses have character.

Violet emerges from her house, balancing a gym bag and foam roller.

Here the flowers bloom all year round.

Violet hums as her feet tap their way down to the car – a small, cardboard-coloured little thing. She packs her things in, then slides into the driver's seat. She smiles a farewell at her standalone house as she backs out of the driveway.

At the bottom, she pauses as she puts the car in gear. The front door opens and Vincent steps out, Charlie scampering around his legs. Violet drives, her gaze split between the road and the rear-view mirror, where she sees Vincent waving her off.

Violet is still smiling when she turns onto Baxter Road.

She's still smiling when she passes the dented pole. For a moment, she almost forgets to give it a sad look that nobody else can see. But then she remembers, and her smile falters.

She comes to a stop at a red light and waits for the stream of cars to flow onto Baxter Road.

The rear-view mirror glints with a splash of sunlight, but Violet keeps her eyes trained on the traffic before her.

Behind her the road curves away to a different time, but now she glances down at herself – her training gear, her tights, and smiles at the anticipation of aching calves and the rhythm of children's laughter.

The light turns green and Violet drives on.

Street Chasers of the
Great South East

Nick van Buuren

'Cadets, if you can handle it, there's good money to be made here.' The site manager was repeating himself. Only this time he added a grandiose sweep of the arm above our heads as if to make himself perfectly clear that by here he not only meant the newly cleared footprint of the *Melaleuca Downs* estate but also some far greater state of affairs.

'Yes, the hours are long and the situation strange,' he continued. An audible chuckle went through the group of men behind me.

Each of them was dressed in the Company's nationally recognisable uniform: a unique cross of paramilitary chic (combat boots, fitted cargo pants and utility belts) with construction site high-vis.

'I want to be entirely upfront and visible about that. Many of you will have done security work before, but it won't have been anything like this.' A second round of laughter came from the old hands, although audibly quieter than the first. The site manager's philosophising clearly had its limits. As he continued, I looked past him to where the sun was falling. Long shadows reached out over the site's boundary from the tree line. Cheers drifted across from the construction teams who had just knocked off and were already drinking by their dormant machinery. The night watch was overdue to start.

'Harvey, Jacobs, Kleinschmidt, Lay, Logan, Masei, Mitgang, Olsen, Pfeilsticker...' I snapped back to attention at the mention of my name.

'Partner up. For your first project you're, officially speaking, "in-training" and to be supervised at all times on-site. And until our next contract comes through you're all sharing each other's kit. Everyone on-site's got to be visible.' A groan arose from the combined crowd, cadets and watchers alike.

'No complaints! If you do your job and you do it well there'll be plenty more streets to watch. Certain as day follows night.'

They put me with Olsen, one of the first watchers. But green as I was and prone to taking everything as given, I didn't recognise the outward signs that implied his experience as a seasoned watcher was from a time pre-privatised before the cut-backs. A near hunchbacked raised shoulder slump, the slowly circling scan of eyes always on watch. All I saw at the time (all I knew how to see) was the resigned look on the site manager's face when he called Olsen's name.

All I heard were sniggers from an unseen corner of the crowd.

With trepidation, I approached the hunched and weathered man. His silver bushman's beard obscured his face. When I held out my hand to greet him, he simply placed a bundled rain poncho into my open palm.

'Less is more. Nothing is Everything. Anything else is Visible,' he said in a foreign accent, unplaceable after what sounded like years of naturalisation.

'Olsen's-Bloody-Maxim,' groaned another seasoned watcher standing beside us. But neither he nor Olsen elaborated any further. Olsen simply turned and walked away from the group. Eventually, I found him where I too was meant to be, at our post at one end of *Proposed Paterson Street*. There we sat through the night, watching.

***

That first night on watch with Olsen was a firm translation of his so-called maxim into measured patience. Despite my eagerness to start some part of the on-the-job training that the recruitment ads had promised, Olsen would not answer my questions directly. Instead, he sat illuminated by the firelight of the barrel between us and simply nodded or would occasionally grunt in response to my anxious enquiries, doing no more or less than acknowledge. Once I had worn myself out after some hours he took the opportunity to ask his own clipped questions.

'What do you do?'

'What do you mean?' The answer seemed obvious given where we were but Olsen's expectant silence seemed to suggest otherwise. 'Uhm, for a while I studied but now I'm here, I guess.'

'What did you study?'

'European History and Languages.'

'Did you finish?'

I was unsure how to answer. The Company's classifieds had been one of the few that didn't require a degree. 'No. I had one semester to go but had to find work.'

Olsen sat silently.

'It's been a long time since we've had an educated cadet on site,' he finally said, then continued, 'watching used to be something people aspired to. Listen carefully tonight. There won't be another chance. Less is more.'

This is how Olsen came to tell me about THE MANUAL. Not knowing any better at the time, I thought Olsen was simply running through the Company onboarding. He talked about THE MANUAL as if it were the common law of the land, the unquestionable ground rules as given to any watcher as the air they breathe. It was only much later, sitting chatting with other cadets in the morning mess tent, breakfast being one of the few luxuries the Company provided, that I realised Olsen, even if for one night only, stepped off the official line and into some long lost past.

As Olsen told it, THE MANUAL was an encyclopaedic account of a watcher's role at work and in society; something every onboarding cadet had once received along with two weeks of study leave and a complete uniform. Olsen, as a young cadet, had read THE MANUAL avidly. Encouraged by THE MANUAL's socially conscious ethic of public service and care that guided a watcher through complex economic and political times, Olsen would lie awake whole days reading THE MANUAL cover to cover before sitting through the night watch fuelled by the electric charge of ideas he'd just taken on.

Guiding me through my introduction of THE MANUAL, Olsen recalled verbatim entire chapters, long tracts dedicated to an honourable lineage of watchers in history: Roman sentries, remote bushfire lookouts, lighthouse keepers and guardian angels. His words became an endless rope of magician's coloured handkerchiefs tied from one corner to the next. Little did I know it was an education that the Company's management had long ago determined could not be afforded to any future watchers to-be.

By the time Olsen's lecture arrived in the watchers' immediate history, he had already been speaking for hours. He paused only to shift forward in his chair, throw more deadwood into the barrel, and then quietly scanned the night around us as the fire caught on again and flared. Other watchers' fires stood out like islands on a dark horizon. Indiscernible chatter drifted across from one direction. A fit of barking coughs punched out of the darkness from the other.

'This is what you must know,' Olsen continued, 'This is nothing to most watchers now. But Nothing is Everything.'

The first watchers had been an enterprising group of security contractors looking to diversify out of the violent and virus-riddled detention and entertainment industries. Their chance came when a series of local governments, gripped by populist fervour, passed the *Uniform Street Names Act 2024* into law.

The Act provided that all citizens possessed a legally enforceable right to name streets as they chose if certain conditions were met. The street had to be a new and previously unnamed public street: not an old road re-laid or a private road for which the landowner retained all naming rights. Most importantly, the individual claiming naming rights had to be the first legal person to have set foot on the newly completed street. As Olsen went through these elements I took out a small notepad and pen. I'd been expecting exactly this kind of introduction on my first shift.

'What are you doing?'

'Taking notes. I can't remember all – '

'No.' Olsen swiftly took the pad from my hand and threw it into the fire. 'Anything that stops us from watching, let alone quotations of THE MANUAL, is contraband on-site. No phones. No books. No pens. No paper. If the site manager so much as saw 'MANUAL' written out in your hand you'd be out of here before the night was done. Just listen. Anything else is Visible.'

What constitutes a 'complete' road was one of the most heavily litigated questions of law in the decade that followed the Act passing. That was until the High Court settled the matter in its watershed decision *Ipswich City Council v Rhodes*. Justice Williams' closing pronouncement from that case is cited as the preferred test: 'Only when one can place one's foot to the road and leave no discernible mark or impression on its surface has the road passed from a state of incomplete to complete, private enterprise to public way.' Olsen's eyes widened as he quoted her Honour's words. His lips gently pushed them out into the air as if he were afraid of breaking them and the power they contained if repeated wrong.

Rhodes was the final say in a long line of litigation instigated by local councils against a then budding cottage industry of serial, semi-professional and hobbyist street namers venomously labelled by the tabloids of the day as Street Chasers. Olsen stood, suddenly erect, hands raised to the lectern of the bar table, paused a moment to shift the weight of his imaginary wig and robes, then earnestly submitted to their Honours the well-known argument of an eminent Queen's Counsel in the cause: 'whereas legislators clearly intended that individuals might be granted such a right so as to name a permanent place in honour of a cherished loved one, admired personage, or dearly missed pet; it is clearly not within the intention of the Acts that they be used as a basis for commercial opportunity, advertising, political broadcasting or otherwise.' Much later, another old hand at street watching, Homer, would tell me that a younger Olsen and he had watched the tape of this particular QC's submissions together on repeat for months. That was until what was art to one became a drinking game to the other and the whole thing grew too painful.

On this question of legislative intention, among the many questions *Rhodes* raised, the court reserved its judgement – holding that it was well within any council's powers to legislate its intentions more clearly. However, in the aftermath of *Rhodes*, councils remained petrified of popular opinion or being seen to be restricting their constituents' rights. The court's long shadow had the opposite effect to that intended by its litigants. Before *Rhodes*, street chasing had been an entirely private affair. But the decision had galvanised it into a legitimate counter-cultural identity. Forums and lobby groups formed. Street chasing tours thrived. The next election was always too close on the horizon for any government to legislate unafraid of popular reprisal at the ballot box.

In time, councils gradually grew accustomed to the appearance of discourse that a free market of street names created. The occasional reclamation by First Nation's people or greyed greenies speaking on behalf of the environment became desirable to many who aspired to the vague neutrality and power of not being considered a bigot. For those playing a longer game, it spoke to a distant hope that an area might quickly pass through boom, bust and dereliction to arrive seamlessly at gentrification where such names might even take on an inherent air of authenticity as if the streets always were and always would be named so. It was only the menace serial namers, or even worse the trolls, that still concerned councils. They were what businesses like the Company were founded to watch out for and keep away from vulnerable unnamed streets.

'But what difference does it make?' I interrupted, 'I mean, a name is a name, what difference does a troll's idea of a name make to any other?'

'Absurdity,' said Olsen immediately.

'Absurdity?'

'Yes, absurdity,' he repeated with the assurance of someone who had never considered that another answer was even possible.

'It pulls the floor out from underneath us all.' At this point, grey light was breaking out over the hills above us. Behind Olsen, the cleared ground between each watcher's camp was becoming visible again.

'Enough,' said Olsen. He nodded over my shoulder to the site manager's distant figure marching from barrel to barrel dismissing watchers from their posts as he went.

'Less is More. Nothing is Everything. Anything else is Visible.' As Olsen repeated his mantra he drew a layer of ash and sand across the smouldering coals of our barrel, folded our chairs then stood at attention waiting.

'Pay comes through on Monday. They want to make sure you turn up for the weekend.' It was the last thing Olsen ever said to me.

***

When I returned for my watch the next night I was met at the gate by the site manager. I was being rotated to my next supervisor early on account of having already shown significant 'promise.' I was flattered, naïve, and had no sense that my move might have had more to do with Olsen's transgression the night before than my own abilities. It was no more visible to me on my second night than it had been on my first that Olsen's trust meant the site manager's distrust. Nor would it dawn on me until well after my time at *Melaleuca Downs* that by placing me with someone like Innes (who never had a pupil before or after me) the site manager was openly admitting to anyone capable of seeing that the Company couldn't afford to let me, or anyone else, go once the work had begun. Less is More. Nothing is Everything. Anything else is Visible.

For weeks I followed my new supervisor Innes around *Proposed Hanson Avenue* with the same earnest intent that I had followed Olsen's words on that first night. And to Innes' credit, each night he would point out the development's progress: where proposed streets had been levelled and grated, the occasional spray-painted dot or dash used to mark where more work was to be done. These were the motions by which suburban sprawl extended its hard edge into unoccupied pasture and bush. They were also the first signs, so he said, that a street chaser looks for when staking out a possible hit.

But quickly Innes' 'methods' stood out against the on-site norm. For instance, he insisted that instead of sitting the night out by our barrel, we should sit with our own fires at opposite ends of *Proposed Hanson Avenue*, changing between the two on the hour like sentries.

'If I was the one planning a sting on this shithole, I'd be watching all these arseholes from up there,' he said pointing above us to a bush-clad ridgeline. The ridge stood silhouetted against a lume-filled night sky and marked the southernmost boundary of clearable country within the city's limits. Soon the town planners and developers would be required to leave the coast and look west for more wide open space. But to Innes, between constant cans of energy drink, chocolate bars and his limitless ability to imagine anyone to be an enemy, that ridgeline marked a hostile frontier.

'What I'd do is wait it out, watch, visualise every step of the approach. It's the fucking *Art of War.* You gotta think like the enemy, see like the enemy and then fuck with them.' Innes elaborated on his strategies each time we swapped from one end of *Hanson* to the other. In the blissful silences that followed his crazed explanations I'd look around at the shadows of men around me, rigid and ballooning in their chairs, wishing the cold nights, months, and years away. I wondered what kind of war Innes thought we were fighting. Weeks of watching quickly became months as I wondered.

I'd have thought Innes and his war were just paranoia if our nights weren't occasionally interrupted by a strange light tracing the ridge or a chilling 'Cooooooooooo-eeeeeeeeeee' rocketing out of the gulley below like the distant cry of some demonic bird. Everyone had their own explanations: kids, folkies, rooting koalas, cats or dogs gone feral. Innes had his war. Each time we passed after such mysterious events he would grab at my arm and hiss: 'that's them, Harvey. *That's them.*'

***

What Innes lacked in reserve and perspective he made up for in eccentricity and an exhaustive knowledge of the latest and greatest Company gossip. As my anaemic cadetship with him continued, he took every opportunity he could to cut my education with rumours and half-truths.

Through his tirades, I learnt a watcher's topography that no map could chart. I saw the precarious place (for now found at *Melaleuca Downs*) where watchers sat, always just barely in touch with the rest of the world. A place that had been a boon for some and a refuge for others. See Homer, the repentant alcoholic who was saved by a sobering combination of night shifts and the Company's blow-zero policy. Or Olsen who, rumour said, was picked up in the Company's fledgling years as part of a Government visa concession scheme for overstayed Danes in the panicked years of worker shortages during the Second Great Sprawl. Although Innes always delivered his stories with a distinct air of contempt, I was always hungry for more and inevitably provided an eager audience.

He would never share his whispers with me on shift or site.

'Too many eyes and ears,' he would whisper.

Instead, I would have to wait until the morning after a particularly uneventful shift, when Innes would predictably reveal that we had been given special orders to work overtime and conduct a reconnaissance trip up to the ridge above *Melaleuca Downs*. I always obliged. Half out of curiosity, half out of fear of refusing Innes although no one else on sight was ever assigned a similarly special and out-of-hours mission. On one of those mornings, halfway up an overgrown and unnamed gulley, I thought to test my luck with Innes.

'Innes, have you read THE MANUAL?'

'Why the fuck would I have read THE MANUAL?' He grabbed a low-hanging branch of blackwood, snapped it off and fashioned it into a switch.

'Even if I wanted to, why would I? THE MANUAL was just some piece of paper for all the old farts that couldn't tell their own arsehole from their faces.'

We reached the gully head, but before I could scramble up onto the loose rock and dust of the ridge line where Innes stood, he turned around accusingly above me.

'What's it matter to you anyway?'

'Nothing. Just heard some talk around the mess tent and was wondering, I guess,' I said.

'Did Olsen tell you anything about THE MANUAL?'

'Maybe in passing.'

'Typical-Fucking-Olsen.' Innes' eyes glared down at me through rivulets of sweat.

'You know Olsen's the reason they got rid of THE MANUAL in the first place.'

'I-uh....' As I grasped for words I could feel myself shrivelling under Innes' unusually intense and focused gaze.

'Management had to axe it 'cos Olsen and his mates got too high-minded 'bout the whole fuckin' thing to 'member how to do their fuckin' jobs. Imagin' that. Getting all educated on the boss' dollar, then spending your whole watch "discoursing" the rights of *the one against the many, the represented against the self-representin'.* Horseshit. The lot of it. One moment they're *inter-lect-tuals.* Then next thing you know. BANG!' Innes clapped his hands together millimetres in front of my face for added effect.

'Fuck me, I wish I could have seen it. One night all the mums and dads are ready to move in. Only thing to be done is name a few streets. Simple. Next thing you know there's so many Beaver Boulevards and Slit Streets in the same postcode that you could have called the place Cunt City.' Innes howled with laughter at his own joke before turning to walk on.

'That's why you don't see Olsen's kind 'round here no more,' he continued as he went, ' 'cos they lost IT. Most of them at the same fucking time.'

'Lost what?' I called after him, making to follow.

'IT! The plot. Their jobs. IT.'

'What?'

'IT!' he shouted back as he stopped at a dry tree limb fallen across the path. He lifted up his right boot as if it were a heavy weapon. 'IT! IT! IT! IT!' he repeated, bringing his foot down with a sickening crack, then again and again until there was nothing left but a mess of broken limbs and splinters. 'THE-KILLER-FUCKING-INSTINCT, HARVEY!' Innes' chest heaved. His shirt was now completely drenched, transparent, and clinging to his body.

'You lose your instinct and next thing you know some kook arsehole who thinks people want to know his dead bitch of a wife's name has got your street by the balls. Don't let Olsen tell you otherwise, Harvey. By the end of it, all the developers couldn't even give the lots away. Whole place tanked. A fucking quack junky dive within the year and it nearly sent the Company broke when the big money came looking for heads to roll. Olsen's just lucky his street was last of the lot and the alarm was raised before anyone hit him. Only fuckin rule at the Company now is that if your street goes, you go.'

Innes walked on again and we continued along the ridge in silence. Eventually, we came to a high point where the low-lying scrub was cleared away leaving only the sparse trunks of tallowwood and a rare few thicker gums. Innes lifted one arm and pointed down below us. From the peak, *Melaleuca Downs* stood in full sight. Its cross-hatched face, across which the morning graters and rollers were already running, stood distinct at the end of a long suburban corridor that led back to the distant heads of high-rises on the hazy horizon.

'Ain't no fucking way that's going to be me, Harvey.' To one side of the site a line of cars crawled away like a retreating trail of ants. It was our fellow watchers knocking off. As each turned from the site's dirt entrance onto the new bitumen of a soon-to-be arterial road, a flash of white light reached us, the sun caught in their windshields.

'Ain't no fucking way no chasers gonna get my street before I get them.'

I stood mesmerised by the pulsing light, thinking in that moment how easily someone might mistake us for being at the source and not the edge of everything below us. I was above it and untouched by Innes' words until the second he struck me with his switch.

'You listening?'

The pain was sudden and stinging. Innes laughed and pointed the switch behind us down the other side of the ridgeline. Loose rocky ground fell away into yet another impenetrable gully, an endless screen of lantana and then endless more ridges and gullies repeating in the same dense pattern behind. But before that in the hollow of a burnt-out eucalyptus lay a mitten of sun-bleached cans and wrappers. The ground beside it had been cleared of rocks and leaf litter. There was room enough for a single person to lie there, invisible to the world below them.

'Ain't no fuckin' way,' Innes repeated, 'I'm a fucking killer.'

***

Two nights later, Innes hospitalised a bushwalker. The poor man had been unfortunate enough to come off the trail and follow his bearing out of the bush and straight onto *Proposed Hanson Avenue*. Initially, it was all excitement. Shouts and floodlights. The sudden buzz of something finally happening. But when we all arrived to see the cast aside backpack and a pair of innocuous boots and gaiters between Innes' straddling legs, the atmosphere quickly fizzled out. An ambulance was called. Someone pulled Innes off and whisked him away.

Those of us left stood silently around the pummelled bushwalker, unsure what to do next. The man's luridly coloured jacket was too bright under the floodlights. It was the first time the emergency lights had been used since us cadets began and our eyes couldn't adjust. Then Olsen broke out of the crowded stupor from nowhere and shouted to all the watchers: 'Back up your streets!' He crouched beside the bloodied naturalist, propped his listless head up on one knee and dabbed at the walker's face with a handkerchief. I tried pushing forward to Olsen's side but a broad arm held me back. The crowd remained set around the veteran and his charge.

'Go! Up your streets!' he shouted with a look of utter disdain before returning his attention to the walker. He cooed, rocked gently back and forth and swept a matted lock of hair away from the walker's face. Then, almost inaudibly he started humming. The bushwalker groaned. Olsen patted him lightly, hushed him as he would a fitful child and then went on humming.

'*Hmmm hmm hmm hmmmm, Hmmm hmm hmm hmmmm.*'

A hand came down and drew me back through the crowd. It was the site manager. He led me without a word back to his demountable office where the air conditioner was running full-pelt despite how cold the nights had been. The site manager was sweating profusely, his red eyes suggested that he had not been able to escape far into a sleep from this watch.

'Cadet…' he paused checking the file in front of him, 'Harvey. You're clearly aware that there has been an incident.' A new well of sweat blossomed at the centre of his shirt. 'I want to be entirely upfront and visible with you about that.' Within seconds two more sweat patches from his armpits reached out and joined the one on his chest.

'You don't need to worry about Innes. He's one of our best and he'll be okay. But he won't be around to supervise you for the rest of your cadetship at *Melaleuca Downs*.' He looked genuinely pained on my behalf. 'And given how far along the project is, this puts us in a bit of a pickle. The pavers are coming in next week and after that we're naming streets. I've had the councillor booked in for months. And as soon as we're wrapped here, we're breaking soil and setting down our chairs in Laidley.'

'Again, being entirely visible with you… Harvey, that timeline can't break. We've got two weeks here with no more time, no more budget, no more watchers hanging around to take your hand. You see my problem?' he paused, and only continued when I slowly nodded in reply.

'Here's what we're going to do. Your cadetship is complete as of tonight. Congratulations, good for you. Now you're changing streets with Jones and his cadet. You'll take Ramsay Street and they'll take Hanson. Ramsay is last on the list to be named so you shouldn't cop any heat.'

'Sir–'

'What. What is it?'

'Sir, I don't think I've enough experience to take on a street of my own. I – '

'Don't overthink it, Harvey,' he cut across, 'you're the cream of the crop!'

'But sir, not even Olsen or Innes have had their own streets. No one has for years. Not since Cu – ' The words, thankfully, caught in my throat.

'Quit it, Harvey,' he said, staring down his nose at me.

'You're in no position to leave. Your sorry arse is HELP loaned up to its eyeballs. Your poor mum's barely qualifying for the dole and your cock-for-brains dad is so far in with the sharks at Queen's Wharf that he has to break a leg just to breathe! I've got friends, Harvey. I've seen your repayment plan. And without your flavour of the month degree, you're not going to get a better deal than this. With any luck, you'll only be here for years not decades. You can't afford not to be.'

My eyes itched and burned as tears welled and then dried under the aircon's blast.

'So, while I'm being entirely visible with you, Harvey, I'd suggest you go home, get some rest and come back here tomorrow night like all you've ever wanted from life was to watch *Ramsay Street*. Am I clear?'

'Yes sir.'

'Good, now make sure you help yourself to a full kit from the locker on your way out. We need you to be entirely visible.'

***

Those last weeks on-site watching *Proposed Ramsay Street*, I got my hunch. With most watchers, the hunch comes on gradually after years of holding yourself through endless cold nights. But there was something about *Ramsay* that brought it all on much quicker than anyone would have expected.

From the strategic bird's eye view, *Proposed Ramsay Street* hooked out into the bush like a curled finger. Being the last street of the lot, a culd-de-sac at the end of, and perpendicular to *Melaleuca Downs'* other street, *Ramsay's* dead-end protruded out into the steep bush surrounding it like the estate's own extended finger. Surrounded by tall stands in all directions bar that from which you came, it made you grip at yourself just to be there.

Every night I felt my shoulders creeping closer and closer to my ears. Though in the bleary-eyed morning when I would escape home for a few restless hours of rest, any change to my posture was imperceptible in the mirror. It was like trying to catch a tree out in the act of growing.

By the time *Melaleuca Downs'* first streets were being named, I found it almost impossible to stand amongst all the fanfare without my shoulders raised, clavicles pressed to my throat. The final laying and naming process was itself a drawn-out affair. The risk of mobs meant that the last layers of bitumen were held off and laid one street at a time under ever anxious and watchful eyes.

First thing the next morning, the council would host a naming ceremony. A trusted delegate of the day would test the surface and turn to the always recording cameras to clearly state the legislatively prescribed phrase: 'I swear, to the best of my knowledge and belief, that the contents of this film are true and correct. I stand here on [*insert desired Street name*] or so help me God.' The delegate would then take a symbolic first step onto the newly named street.

As a matter of professional custom, we watchers stayed on after each night shift to witness and applaud another street safely named. The agonising mundanity of watching yet another honoured guest state their oath for the cameras might have ended the tradition by now (watchers not being known for their sentimentality) if these mornings weren't also our last chance to see that street's watcher until the final name and big reveal of our next watching site. The Company didn't keep us on any longer than it needed to.

Paterson Street had been amongst the first streets named and as I watched Olsen walk away off-site I imagined myself by his side, newly graduated from my cadetship, and leaving this shithole behind, however briefly, until we returned to watch some new and indistinguishable scar upon the land. But in the present, as each subsequent street was finished, our morning huddle of watchers grew smaller and smaller. Those of us that remained grew increasingly anxious. We knew we could only cheat fate for so long. Meanwhile, the councilmen became increasingly jubilant. How long had it been since so many streets were named according to plan?

What those sleepers didn't see, but we watchers did, were the ever-increasing nocturnal activities closing in on us, occurrences that we at first had only regarded with light superstition but now saw to be sure omens of an impending apocalypse. Lights that had once been only momentary flashes above our heads were now defiant burns along the ridgeline lasting the whole night. No one yarned by their barrels anymore but the ceaseless sounds of half-heard conversations remained. Again and again, the ghostly cries sounded that could have been either a bird or a crying child. The brittle rhythm of something walking across dry and crackling leaf litter. In the amphitheatre-like arena of *Proposed Ramsay Street*, those night noises combined into the feeling that someone was always out there, pacing a great arch from one side to the other like a stalking cat.

By the time only five of us remained to clap along the final week of predictable tears of yet another honoured war widower, I could barely sleep through the day. Each new watch was a waking nightmare. *Proposed Ramsay Street* was due to be named on Saturday morning and our first street fell on Wednesday night.

I saw the first flash from my post. Then, running across site, I saw by the light of a second flash the silhouette of a small child standing on Homer's newly set road. Darkness returned but the child's figure remained burnt into the night ahead of me. Then a third flash revealed the camera and tripod, someone standing behind it, and behind them two men holding Homer in a press. One with his hand over the old watcher's mouth. I reached them only as everyone broke from their frieze. Homer stood slumped. The man who'd been gagging him walked over with a cheer to pick up the child.

'We did it, baby!'

'Spot!' shouted the child. It was a young girl wearing the tiara and dress of a princess over her flannelette pyjamas. She giggled and cheered with her father. A woman came out from behind the camera and ran over to join them.

The other man simply stood beside the dejected watcher and looked on.

'Nothing personal, mate. We couldn't get her to stop crying,' he said, raising a hand to Homer's back. 'She really loved that dog.'

It was the way he then patted Homer that finally got to me. I shouted and stepped around to push him off of Homer.

'Go on, fuck off the lot of you.' I was angry. One more day on *Melaleuca Downs* would have made for Homer's 15 years of sober watching.

The man barely stumbled. 'You right, mate?' He squared up and stood to his full height. Any fire I'd had in me immediately fell away. He sensed it too and I saw in his eyes something that reminded me of Innes.

'I said f-fuck off.' The words barely got past my trembling lip.

The man smiled darkly.

'Oi!' The other man appeared between us with his daughter still in his arms. 'Leave it. There's a kid here.' He then turned directly to me and the other watchers who had just arrived to add, 'you fellas go on have a good night. It's nothing personal.'

That morning we boycotted the naming of *Spot Street*. Whether it was in mourning or protest was unclear, but we knew we'd never see Homer again – not at this site or the next. He'd disappeared before the site manager could even arrive to do up his exit report and he left only a small pile of belongings exactly where he'd been arrested by the chasers. He'd asked me that they be distributed between the remaining watchers on-site but the site manager quickly requisitioned the equipment as soon as he saw it. Although, I'd managed to grab a head torch before that.

As I walked off-shift I could see the ceremony going ahead as normal without us, rolling through the routine acknowledgement of country and subsequent acknowledgement of honoured guests. The councillor gave a relieved smile to the cameras as he shook the naming girl's hand.

'Spot!' called the gathered crowd in the photographer's direction. A council worker climbed his ladder and went to work placing letters, pausing a moment, then sighing heavily and pulling out a palette knife to scrape away the *b* he'd mistakenly placed as a reversed *p*.

***

On my final night, the place was deserted. The site manager had made it clear he couldn't find the budget or care to put on extra watchers. It was also the first Friday night off for most since *Melaleuca Downs* broke ground. No one was spending the night with me out of sympathy or stupidity.

At the gate, lifting the padlock and drawing through the gate's heavy chains, the site manager already smelled like a bar rag.

'Hold it, Harvey,' he called after I'd already walked past with downturned eyes. He pulled out a bright orange snub-nose revolver and pointed it at me. We stood frozen, a grim expression on the site manager's face for a second until it cracked into a stupid grin.

'Don't look so shocked, Harvey!' He keeled over laughing. 'It's only a flare,' he said wheezing.

When he straightened I saw that he'd yet again brought himself to tears.

'Figured tonight you might care for some extra *enlightenment*,' he continued, setting himself off in another fit. He threw the flare gun to the ground in front of me and pulled the gates shut still laughing.

The surfacing labourers had been to *Proposed Ramsay Street* that afternoon. My eyes itched from the fumes coming off the setting bitumen. I pressed the toe of my boot down on the street's edge then pulled away to reveal a perfect impression of its patterned tread. Taking a seat beside my barrel, I started the fire and faced the wall of bush that surrounded me. Long shadows of tall standing tallow and rosewood reached out from the darkening hillside as night arrived.

If there were street chasers out there watching me, I didn't see them until well after midnight. A low cloud had covered the waxing moon. While my eyes adjusted, their first faint footsteps must have been so slight that I didn't hear them over the fire's crackle. But then that first crunch of leaf litter followed closely by the hissing rush of soil and sand, sticks and leaves sliding underweight.

Things always sound closer than they are. Noise carries in these gullies. I had plenty of time. But all the same, I did a quick round of *Proposed*

Ramsay's perimeter, collecting deadwood as I went. When I sat back down with my load and looked up, a single pinprick of light, a lone star in the night, had appeared halfway up the dark hill above me.

I repeated my round, this time depositing small caches as I went: a handful of dry eucalyptus leaves, thin fingers of she-oak and their dry needles for flare, thicker knotted limbs to keep things burning. On a dark night like tonight, I was sure that I wouldn't be visible until I chose to be. Looking up I saw that the single star had divided into three duller but distinct lights. They were close enough now that I could see each light waver slightly as it bobbed along its separate course down the gully.

I ran to the far end of *Proposed Ramsay Street* with my lighter and starter fluid, quickly spraying the wood piles until the leaves and limbs were dripping with fuel. Then I trailed a line back to the next pile and then back to the next until I returned to the already stoked and roaring barrel. One more look up at the approaching lights. They were two-thirds of the way down, each now bright and steady. I picked up a loose strip of paperbark and held it over the flames until it caught and then dropped the burning bundle.

I had expected a sudden roar – *whoosh*. But instead, a small quick flame silently traced between piles along the length, width and then length again of *Proposed Ramsay Street*. Each pile looked as if it had barely caught. I ran between each, desperately fanning, begging for something to catch. I ran back to my barrel, grabbed more fistfuls of leaves and kindling, and ran back to the fledgling fires, throwing down the fuel. The piles smoked. I looked up. The lights, not so distant anymore, kept approaching.

I ran back to the barrel one more time to grab the lighter fluid. The closet pile was almost out as I pulled off my jacket, bunched my shirt and poured the remaining fluid out over it, soaked the damn thing, and threw it onto the fire. *Whoomph*.

Everything caught at once. Flames leapt above my head. A wave of heat surged out and made every hair on my bare chest stand on end and then curl. Innes and his blissful madness crossed my mind and I howled at the covered moon.

I walked back to my barrel and took one of the last pieces of solid wood from the stockpile there, a 5ft staff knotted at its head and still a little spring in its length. I strode back to the new bonfire, now roaring, and pushed the staff into its depths, twisted what burning streaks of my shirt remained around it. Then, with a kind of solemn ceremony, I strode from pile to pile in my line of watchtowers. I was the harbinger. I was the risen warrior. As each choked pile roared back into life, I committed another mad howl to the moon.

It was only when I returned to my barrel that I saw the lights had stopped. They hovered on the hillside at the edge of darkness, just beyond the fire's glow. I howled again and threw fistfuls of eucalyptus leaves into the fire. I howled and beat my chest as the fire flared. My eyes adjusted to the new excess of light and trailed down from the perched lights through the silhouetted tree canopy. The long arms and spread fingers of the tallest gums had been transformed into gothic arches. And on the ground below them, flickering in and out of sight as the firelight threw itself against the tree line and then drew back was rank upon rank of ghostly figures watching me from between the trees.

'I see you!' I called across the vacant lots but it was barely true.

At first, one figure was all I could see for sure. The ghost. Its curved shoulder and hip extending from behind the limbs of the grey gum's scared surface barely seemed there. But once seen, more hands and limbs appeared where before there had only been shadows and bush.

'You're entirely visible to me!' I shouted over my shoulder in the other direction where yet more figures were emerging. I drew up the last of the woodpile and made a nervous round, feeding the ravenous fires that had already started to flag. As I went, I counted tens, maybe even hundreds of people now standing out in the open.

'You're too early! You come at it now and you get nothing!' I couldn't read the mob. I was surrounded and two options ran through my mind. Walk off the job now, keep walking and hope docking my bonus gives the site manager and his cronies enough satisfaction to save me ever having to see them again. Or stay. Stay and hope for morning.

'Take a look for yourselves!' I picked up the last remaining piece of timber. It was my scorch-headed and unbroken staff and I walked up to the bell end of *Proposed Ramsay Street*. Stepping up from cleared earth to the road I felt the bitumen still shifting slightly beneath my feet. In two swift movements, I lifted the staff above my head and then drove it down into the street. It stuck straight and tall.

'You see this stick!' I shouted, taking a step back and turning to face the trees. 'So long as this stick stands there's still some give in the road. You haven't got half a chance in hell of naming this street if you come up here before this stick falls.'

A murmur went around the crowd. I could see by the firelight that the mob was breaking up into parties, and these parties in turn folded in on themselves to discuss. How much time had I bought myself? Hell, I'd almost convinced myself with the whole display when a stray voice called out from the dark.

'Bullshit!'

'Who said that?' I spun looking for the culprit. 'Who said that!' I screamed at the unmoving stands. Then the call came again.

'Bullshit!'

This time I would have sworn it came from the opposite side of the street. I marched over, stood on the imagined back fence line and leered into the crowded dark. The voice came again, echoing through the bush and out onto the street.

'Bullllllllllll-shhhhhhhhiiiiiittt.'

A wide figure had emerged across the street from me and stopped at the opposing fence line. As the echo faded it rocked forward and straightened at the knees to reveal two bright and dancing opaque prisms of firelight where there should have been eyes. A balaclava pulled tightly down over the neck and tucked into stretched fatigues obscured its face.

'You're all on your own,' they said in a softer but emboldened voice. 'You're all bluff!' they spat.

'Even if that stick meant shit, there's nothing you'd be able to stop us once it falls.' They took one step forward and the firelight flashed again across their eyes like a nightmare blade. I saw the glinting daylight across car windows seen from on high.

With the next step and another flash, I saw all the other watchers going to leave.

Then another step and I felt Innes' violence once more beside me in an otherwise beautiful and indifferent place. And another, that violence rising up inside me.

The figure's steps rolled into each other as they built up momentum. A branch cracked as more people stepped out into the clear.

'Stop!' I cried as the figure reached halfway to the front fence. But they still kept coming. The crowd was moving too, merged once more into a surging mob.

'I – said – STOP!' There was a gun in my hand, pointed squarely at the ghoul. Everything froze. They took a moment before I recognised the site manager's flare gun.

'*Wooooow*, man. No need to let things get out of hand.' But even as they spoke I watched my own thumb rise of its own mind and pull back the gun's hammer. Even below the balaclava, I could see a face crumpling.

'If anyone even has a go before *this* stick falls…' I shouted in a voice I didn't recognise as my own. 'If anyone so much as *moves*…' I took a step forward on the last word and watched as the world stepped back.

'Then I'm not afraid to use this.' The gun lifted over my head momentarily for all to see. A grumble rolled around the cul-de-sac. Some onlookers turned and disappeared into the bush, shaking their heads at the sudden change in rules.

The gun's sights returned to the masked figure still standing where they had frozen.

'Come on, man,' they whimpered, 'it's only a street. I didn't mean anything by it.' Their glasses were now askew. I felt a faint satisfaction seeing that their eyes were streaming, their top lip barely able to stay in place as the begging started. 'Come on, man, I was only doing what everyone does.'

'Go!' I shouted. But the chaser was stunned and stayed put despite the terror in their eyes. I could see a dark patch spreading across its pants. 'Go!' I roared again.

'Go! Go! Go!' I lunged forward and the chaser wailed then ran. 'Go! Get! Go on before I blow your fucking brains out!' I ran a few more steps barking like a dog until the chaser escaped past the others and disappeared into the scrub.

Another grumble and a few tut-tuts of disapproval followed me as I walked back to my barrel and sat down cross-legged, one eye on my still standing yardstick and the other on the remaining chasers. The majority of the crowd stayed but had taken a seat, resigned to their new roles as spectators.

I looked down at my watch. Two hours to dawn and maybe another hour after that until the council arrived. Would anyone have called the police? Not yet. That would shut things down and then no one would get a shot at the street. No, two hours until dawn.

'Fucking try me.'

An hour later the fires died. I sat and watched as my illuminated perimeter retreated and the crowd advanced their camp, always just beyond the edge of darkness. Occasionally, I'd pull out Homer's headtorch to throw a spotlight onto some unsuspecting crawler. They'd freeze in the sudden light and I'd leave the light on them just long enough to keep the sharp edge of panic pressing. In those moments I was as much a killer as anyone. But once I pulled the light off, I felt myself immediately diminish. It took minutes for my eyes to adjust enough to see even my own hands. And from that point, all I could see of the chasers surrounding me were ghostly half figures and impressions: a headless torso floating by from one end of the street to the other only for its lost head to come back in the other direction.

I jerk upright as I watched the head down the street. Felt myself slipping in and out of sleep as it was swallowed by murky darkness. The cloud cover came and went, revealing the moon upon a fresh perch each time. In those moments *Ramsay Street* lay unblemished and silver until out of the shadowy wings, a curlew stepped. It was the first I'd seen at *Melaleuca Downs* despite the many I'd heard over the months. The bird stood in the middle of the street under the moon's spotlight, stretching its wings. Every time its haunting cry entered me and ricocheted within my chest. A moment later the clouds fell back together and the street returned to darkness, my curlew out of sight.

I quietly crawled out from my post beside the still standing staff to where the curlew had been. No trace. No mark. No impression or indentation. Still prone I ran my hand back and forth across the site. I pressed my own palm down to the bitumen. Not even a dent.

***

With dawn came the familiar sound of chains running across wire, the groan of gates opening. Not one of my fellow watchers would have expected what they found as they came across the site together, a ragtag battalion, at the behest of the site manager's proclivity for pomp and ceremony. But what exactly had I hoped for? An armed escort? Charging cavalry? Divine intervention? They were all back at the site manger's behest to put on a final great show of force before the council at what was to be the last naming and hopefully the execution of a new contract. But with no hope or prospect of any improved circumstances with the move from one site to the next, the collected watchers made for a lacklustre parade.

Then, at the sight of the thousands of chasers that had arrived overnight, the absurdity of their situation broke on the watchers like a wave. One laughed. Soon the whole line was keeling over. Amongst the crowd of chasers, where there had initially been a few anxious looks at the arrival of uniformed men, the laughter caught on, first in spot fires then as a roaring front that encircled the street.

Still laughing, the watchers broke ranks. Friends and relations recognised one another and embraced. Others walked amongst each other still twitchy and nervous, some red-eyed or nursing sleeping children. But the children soon woke and the watchers welcomed them. Chasers in turn asked the watchers to sit and share the pillows and rugs laid down over the site's cut surface.

Soon two crowds were simply one great din. The site manager shouted and swore from the corner of *Proposed Ramsay* and *Hanson*. But he didn't dare step in amongst the throng. Instead, he waved around the road sign he'd brought reading: 'DO NOT STEP. ROAD MAY BE SET.' And when no one took notice of his sign he threw it down and walked back to his demountable, threatening to call the police.

The sun had completely risen over the hills. At the other end of *Proposed Ramsay Street*, where I stood by my barrel and staff bemused, someone pulled out a guitar. The cul-de-sac filled with its tentative strums. Kids ran freely. They fearlessly zig-zagged, with their arms outstretched, across the demilitarised zone I'd created and cheered at each other '*Chaser-chase-Watcher-watch-Watcher-*

chase-Chaser,' until someone was caught and the chant reversed: '*Watcher-chase-Chaser-watch-Chaser-chase-Watcher.'*

TV crews arrived. Their vans followed the already laid roads until the swelling crowd that had now overflowed into *Melaleuca Downs's* other streets stopped them from going any further. Reporters were out and ready for the cross in seconds. Behind them came a convoy, cars and buses carrying the elderly, Rotarians, and Scouts. I thought I even saw the flash of Olsen's face behind the wheel of one mini-bus. But then whatever spectre I'd seen disappeared as the bus turned and its side door spewed out a contingency from the bowls club.

A faint breeze picked up, carrying with it the buzz of the strummed melody. Twists of eucalyptus leaves spun down from the trees. Cans cracked open. Distant sirens faded in and out of earshot as a general humming grew and then broke into sung verses.

Kookaburra sits on the old gum tree,
Merry merry king of the bush is he.

People stood and sang with arms linked, ignoring those reporters that scoured through the crowd for comment.

Laugh, Kookaburra, LAUGH, Kookaburra,
Gay your life must be!

A police patrol car arrived with its lights going. The officers stepped out quickly but advanced no further.

'What was the reported incident?' one officer asked into her radio as the other called for backup.

LAUGH, Kookaburra, LAUGH!

The singing echoed up the gully. It was a drinking song, a nursery rhyme, a football cry.

LAUGH, KOOKABURRA LAUGH!

The line went round and round the crowd, pulling more and more in until thousands were singing. The breeze gusted, throwing up broken earth and ash in miniaturist willy willies.

LAUGH, KOOKABURRA LAUGH!

The hollow clang of timber on bitumen rang out. As I took a step back over the fallen staff and up onto the street all I could see was people: people singing, people dancing, people running towards me.

Kookaburra, gay your life must be.

Contributors

BRIANNA BULLEN writes science fiction short stories about memory. Her poetry chapbook *Unicorns with Unibrows* was published by Puncher & Wattmann, with a second chapbook *Omelettes for Night Owls* forthcoming with Dancing Girl Press.

FREYJA CATRON is an emerging writer from Bundjalung country. She has had her writing published in *Voiceworks*, *Hothouse Literary Journal* and *Dark Mountain*. She's currently spending her time riding horses through the hills of Wales.

MAZ HOWARD is a creative writing student at the University of Adelaide. Their poetry has won the Hachette Australia Prize for Young Writers and been displayed in pavement art through Raining Poetry Adelaide.

PATRICK TAYLOR is a Sydney-based writer with a lifelong passion for literature and screen arts. He loves exploring gothic styles and subject matter, and was recently accepted into the Australian Writers' Guild's inaugural First Break program.

SVETLANA STERLIN writes prose, poetry, and screenplays in *Meanjin*. Her work appears in *Meanjin*, *Cordite*, *Voiceworks*, and elsewhere. A former swimmer, she makes everything about swimming, like her online publication *swim meet lit* mag.

NICK VAN BUUREN is a writer, poet, and editor writing from Meanjin/Brisbane. He has performed with the Queensland Poetry Festival since 2017; published poetry in *Australian Poetry Journal*, *Voiceworks*, and *sugarcane*; and is the co-founder of the darling but now deceased literary zine *The Tundish Review*.

Editors

EMMA WORTLEY has a background in academia and has published papers on children's and young adult literature (the subject of her PhD thesis) in various journals. Her reviews, stories and poetry have appeared in *Voiceworks*, *Southerly*, *Going Down Swinging*, *Paper Crown Magazine*, *textLitmag*, *Scintilla Magazine*, *Scum Mag* and episodes of the *Story Club* podcast.

CH'ASKA CUBA DE REED lives and writes on unceded Gadigal land. Her work has been published in *Scum Mag*, *Slinkies Shorts* and the *UTS Writers Anthology*, amongst others.

Spineless Wonders publications are available in print and digital format from participating bookshops and online. For further information about where to purchase our print and ebooks, go to the Spineless Wonders website:

www.shortaustralianstories.com.au